Logos and Other Stories

Jack Dukes

Copyright 2012 Jack Dukes

ISBN-13: 978-1477685792

Table of Contents

LOGOS	1
The Big Lonely	113
Cutting Lose	121
The Predators	136
Jonathon	166
The Golden Pheasants	181
The Loon & the Tomcat	200
The Red-Tailed Hawks	217
Under a Hunter's Moon	241
Another Time, Another War, Another Mother	265
August 9th, 1930	276
Christmas, 1939	285
Eternal Water	289
Fighting for Fun	293
Grandma, 1935	299
The Backwards Elephant	308
Easter Blossom	313
Blackie	317
Courage	327
Party	335
Soda Jerk	343
Rats	352
Glasses	361

LOGOS

CHAPTER 1

Zilvan's twin sister, Hydilla, closed the airlock behind him. He stepped out into the black emptiness surrounding the Earth orbiting space-city, Logos. He meticulously maneuvered his way through the massive bases of mile-long solar panel arrays until he came to a substation. Anchoring his boots in the restraints, he unsheathed an arm-long wrench and began hammering at every gauge he could reach, some of them bigger than himself. None of them smashed. When he was sure his efforts were folly, he released the restraints and returned through the same airlock. Hydilla helped him out of his suit.

"Success?" she asked.

"Failure," he said.

"I'm glad."

He gave her a mild, pouting look and began stowing the spacesuit components. He worked swiftly while Hydilla listened at the entryway.

"Hurry," she said.

"Done!" he replied and rushed towards her.

She met him halfway. She began kissing him. He did not return her caresses until the entry opened and two Intercessors stepped through. The ICs grinned briefly at the twins, then completed visual and ray scans of the massive girder complex above the walls of the storage area. They looked at each other, shook their heads in the briefest of noes and turned to the twins.

"Did either of you see who used that airlock?" The shorter one, seven-feet plus tall, smiled as he spoke.

Only at the question did the twins stop embracing and face the intruders. Standing hand-in-hand and shoulder-to-shoulder, both of them said no.

"We got here just before you did," added Hydilla, her voice as bright as starlight.

Staring down at Zilvan, the shorter Intercessor stated, "You're curator of The Garden, aren't you? I thought I'd seen you before." Turning to Hydilla, he asked, "Who are you?" He stared first at her, then at him, puzzled by their similar appearances.

"I'm Hydilla. I activate the Inn of Joy."

"An Activator, no less! I'm impressed. I've never been there, but I understand you're pretty good. Do you really do all the things they say you do?"

Hydilla blushed. "It's mostly illusion. Sometimes, with the right partner, it's real, but not very often."

"Yes, well, may we have your numbers, please?"

The twins held their right wrists out for inspection. The shorter IC read the numbers from them into his identifier.

"27539791.a and 27539791.b. Why, you're twins!" he said even before the IDs were returned. "What kind of an act is this? Why were you putting on a show of being lovers?"

"We are lovers," insisted Hydilla. "We are orphans and genetic throwbacks. We have clung to each other from the beginning. You have no law against it, and there's nothing you can do about it."

"They're orphans all right," said the tall one, all of eight feet high. "Axel confirms it. Huh. So this is how Level Niners do things. No wonder more problems come from there than anywhere else. Let's get out of here. We'll report a cosmic and let it go at that. OK with you?"

"OK," said his partner. "As long as you don't think they're the ones...."

His partner interrupted him with a hand on the shoulder and a shove towards the door.

"Nonsense. They're Retros. They don't understand things like airlocks and spacesuits. Don't embarrass them though. They could cause trouble with the Archons."

His voice faded as he walked away. Zilvan's face turned red with the force of his anger.

"Cause trouble," he hissed. "I'll send your precious Logos and King Axel back to Earth where they belong. *Don't understand stuff like spacesuits and airlocks,*" he mocked. "Well, I'm learning, thanks to this." He patted the device strapped to his left wrist. It looked identical to the one Hydilla, and indeed all Logotians wore or had at hand at all times. "Let's go."

"Are you going back to the Garden?" she asked.

"Yes. Want to come along?"

"No, I have to go to the Inn. I'm dancing tonight."

"See you later?"

"Sure."

As they left the storage area, Logos shook as if a giant hand had hammered it. Video and audio alarm systems were going off on all levels. The door slammed shut behind them. A panel beside it flashed a red warning: DANGER – SPACE LEAK. An oddly neutral voice tolled out the dropping pressure in pounds per square inch. The twins unconsciously huddled together as a work crew came racing down the corridor.

"Was anyone in there?" yelled the leader.

"No. We just got out ourselves."

"You're lucky. Everything loose in there has been sucked out into space. You're two damned lucky Retros."

The work crewmembers, like practically all adult Logotians, stood over seven feet tall. Zilvan, less than six feet, barked up at them, "Don't call us Retros!"

They paid him no heed.

"We can't go in through here," said the crew chief. "Let's look at Level Four."

The neutral voice intoned, "Radiation level is 2500 Roentgens."

"Damn," said the chief. "If that thing gets to Axel…." His voice trailed off.

"What happens then?" asked Zilvan.

"If radiation gets to Axel, Logos becomes Heaven and you become angels. Let's go," he said to his crew and they departed on the run.

"Did you hear that, Hydie? I never thought of going after Axel. What an idea! No more space walks. No more banging my heart out on unbreakable gauges. No more having you stand guard for me. I can't believe it. Are you still going to the Inn?"

"I have to. Will you come?"

"No. I have a lot of things to think about. By the way, what made you tell the IC we were lovers?"

"It just popped into my mind."

"Well, it was an inspired lie. Did you see the looks on their faces?"

"Did I! I was afraid I'd laugh out loud."

"Me, too. Hey, Hydie?"

"What?"

"Don't ever lie to me."

Her expression got serious, though the melody stayed in her voice.

"I won't, Zilvan. Not ever."

He smiled. "Give me one."

She pecked his forehead with her lips. He returned the kiss in the same manner. They parted, smiling: he, down the zigzag corridors outlining the pentagram-shaped units that formed the structure of Logos, she, down the people mover, where she was recognized and greeted by most that saw her.

CHAPTER 2

Zilvan didn't need to look at the direction signs that lit up automatically as he approached. He had walked the corridor many times before, thinking, scheming, and building up courage to carry out his next futile attempt to return Logos to Earth. He walked with his head down, not in the dejection of one more failure, but in the manner of deep concentration. He was bathed in the shadowless light that accompanied all movement in the corridors, which lit ahead for six feet and behind for one foot, quitting without a glow once the movement was gone.

He was too abstracted to notice the light approaching him in the same length of corridor. As the two light pods met, a guttural male voice spoke.

"Forehead, Zilvan."

No reply. The approacher stopped and held out a hand to catch Zilvan by the arm. His face was pointed, like an animal's snout, and the teeth he showed were fangs. It was difficult to tell if the expression he showed was a snarl or a grin.

"Forehead, Zilvan."

"What? Oh. Forehead, Rytan. Sorry. I was thinking about something."

"Got anything for trading?"

"Maybe. What would you like?"

"A rabbit?"

"Just happen to have a young, tender one, Rytan."

"What do you want for it?"

"Ohh, I don't know. I really don't need anything. Maybe I'd better keep it. It makes a nice pet. You'd just eat it raw. Tell me, do you kill them before you eat them?"

Rytan's face darkened. "It's my business what I do with them. I suppose you cook yours?" The last remark was a sneer.

"As a matter of fact, I've found a way to do just that."

"I don't believe you," said Rytan and started to walk away.

"Wait, Rytan. I've just thought of something I can use."

Rytan turned immediately and walked back "All right, what?"

"I want supervisor level access to Axel."

"Not a chance." He turned to leave.

"A rabbit a month for three months? Each one bigger than the one before?"

Rytan stopped again. "Six months?"

"Four," said Zilvan. "That's all I can manage to steal from the Garden."

"When do I get the first one?"

"Right now, if you want to come along."

"You're all right, Zilvan. You're all right. But I can't come now. I'm on my way to rehab."

"What for?"

"For being a Masso."

"You? A Masso? I don't believe it. Only Logotians with APM's are Massos. I don't believe you."

For answer, Rytan pulled his shirt up over his chest. From navel to nipples, he was crisscrossed with wounds in various stages, from fresh to scabbing to scarred. While Zilvan watched in disbelief, Rytan cut a new wound, starting at his navel and going down two inches. He used the nail of the little finger of his right hand. The nail was sharpened to a long point and cut effortlessly. Rytan grinned at the expression on Zilvan's face.

"I like it, Zil. I like pain. It's not like the Logotians. They want to only feel pain long enough to activate their anti-pain modules, their APM's. Level Niners, like you and me, don't have those, so I can't stop the pain. I feel it all the way and I like the feelings. That's why I'm not afraid of the reconstruction chambers. For me, it would be like a giant orgasm. It's the only feeling I can count on as real in this orbiting, metallic and plastic space turd. Sometimes, I'm even crazy enough to hope that you succeed in your efforts to bring Logos down. Even if it kills us all. At least it will be real."

"I don't know what to say, Rytan. I can't suck it all in. You've been my friend for ten years, and I never suspected. It's almost like you betrayed me. Maybe you'd better come over after you're done. We need to talk."

"I will, Zilvan. Don't feel betrayed. The subject just never came up, that's all. I would have told you.

"I kiss your forehead, Rytan."

"And I yours."

Without another word, they walked in opposite directions, each alone in his light pod.

CHAPTER 3

To enter his star, Zilvan passed his palm above a scanner. The door opened instantly, soundlessly. Shadowless light filled the interior. Sound patterns sent waves of relief through his body. A voice of sultry perfection petted him. He had spent countless hours perfecting her tone, pitch, and volume.

"Welcome to your star, Zilvan. Your magnetic couch is ready to support you in any position you like. You may have a relaxant, soporific, or euphoric cocktail."

"Relaxant, please."

A panel in the control console from which the voice came, opened. He reached in and extracted a goblet of iridescent blue, filled with liquid amber. The surface shimmered from the slight tremor in his hand as he looked, inhaled the aroma, and drank. He returned the empty goblet. "More," he said. Nothing happened. "More, please."

"I'm sorry, Zilvan. Your quota of relaxant has been consumed. Don't feel disturbed. You will be relaxed in a moment or two."

"You, too, you dumb damned machine."

There was no answer. He kicked the console.

"People think you're so damned perfect, but I know better. You're in a constant state of decay. You've got thousands of Logotians crawling all over you like termites attending a queen. If I could, I'd squash all those little bugs just to watch you die. There's too many for that, though. I hope you scream when you die, Axel. Even if I never hear it, I hope you scream."

He went into the sonic shower without removing his clothing. Massaging waves stripped the sprayed-on material covering his body. Jets of warm water completed the cycle, selected automatically by Axel to meet the specific needs of Zilvan's request for relaxation. He closed his eyes tightly when a spongy material enveloped him, taking up every bit of water from his body. He walked nude to the console in the center of his star.

"I want to think, Axel, please."

"Of course, Zilvan. You are 483 days behind in thought cocktails. How much will you have?"

"A double, please."

The door opened, presenting an orange goblet filled with bright yellow liquid. He drank half of it and then rolled onto the magnetic couch, invisible to the naked eye, at the side of the console. It supported him completely. He lay on his back, his hands near his hips, his knees slightly raised. He spoke to Axel, though his gaze was fastened on the three-dimensional representation of Earthly pastoral tranquility that was the ceiling in the center of his star.

"You know what's the trouble with me, Axel? It's you."

He scratched his head - not as for an itch, but for pleasure, using long, gentle strokes.

"There isn't any way for me to beat you...yet. I know how to manipulate you well enough to have my own private zoo in the Garden, but I don't know how to defeat you."

He rolled onto his side and stared at the console.

"I've got to kill you, Axel. You supply my every need, grant my every desire, you answer all my questions. Yet, you keep me away from my mother Earth."

He drank from the goblet.

"Soon now, I will be up for breeding. I want that to happen more than anything else in my life, even more than killing you. I am the last of my seed. But I need it to happen on Earth. Here, I would never know which child was mine, or which woman the mother. Or even if my union survived. All thanks to you for taking the humanity out of procreation. Cheers."

He sipped at his cocktail after raising it in salute, then rolled back and stared at the ceiling again.

"You monitor my health every time I go to a sanitary station and cure me of ailments before I even know I've got them. You feed me syn-food in whatever form and flavor I want. I can eat all I want of everything I want and not get fat or sick. No wonder Logotians virtually worship you."

He sat up, cross-legged, and drank the rest of his drink. He saluted the console with the empty container.

"I have to kill you Axel, and for that, they will kill me. Death to Axel, death to Zilvan." He threw the glass at the console. It bounced off harmlessly.

"Silly thing to do," he murmured as the relaxant in his drink began to take hold. He rolled off the couch to recover the goblet. "But, that's OK. I need a great anger to destroy you. The more I realize how dependent I am on you, the more I hate you. Another thought cocktail, please."

The console responded to the trigger words "thought" and "please," and produced the beverage immediately. He watched as the liquid poured from a tap into a goblet selected from a rainbow turntable.

"Blue goblet, amber liquid. Orange goblet, yellow liquid. It's always the same. The temperature's the same, the humidity, the movement of air. I hate you for your perfection. And it's no different in the Garden. You control the rain, the population, the balance of everything. Ohh, how I would love to know a thunderstorm! I would stand on a hill under a tall tree and laugh at a forgotten God for the joy of it!

"Hear me, Axel! I will kill you! The Archons say the Earth is bleak, without green life, covered by a never-ending shroud of brown death. But they only know what you tell them, and I think you're wrong…unless they're the ones lying. But why would they do that? I think there are people down there…like me, not like these space-freak Logotians. I must join them or die trying. Another thought cocktail, please."

Zilvan retrieved it, saluted the console, drank the entire potion and sank to one knee, head bowed low.

"But I will not die easily, oh, mighty Axel. Though it is the death of ten thousand failures, I will not surrender nor cry that I cannot go on. So, Axel, kill me now if you hear me. When I arise, I will lie, cheat, steal, and murder to be master of my fate."

As he reached for the console, his hand trembled. Then, suddenly, he placed his palm on it and raised himself to his feet. He began singing:

"White clouds gleam as sunshine streams

To show off blues and greens, together.

Snow and rain are only pain

Until they paint the plains, together.

Someday I, will fall down from the sky

And find my love and I, together."

He continued humming and whistling the tune as he went about cleaning the cages of the black-market animals that lined one arm of his star. Each cage held a single animal: a rabbit, a squirrel, a snake, a bird. Though there was often more than one of an animal, each had its own cage. A sonic barrier prevented any sound from entering the hub of his star. When he opened the cage of a mouse, he found six pink newborns already attached to teats.

"Wonderful, little mother! Feed your babies well. When you stop suckling them, they will be tidbits for the snake, crow, and fox. They will enjoy the fruits of your labor.

"Hello, little fox. How tiny you are. How tiny you all are, less than half of what you should be. Axel's doing again. He took away your right to natural selection and diminished everything about you. I wish you could be an army for me. With your spirit of survival, I could not lose a war."

A sharp beep intruded the noise in the arm. Zilvan went to the console to press a control. The entry screen showed Rytan in a state of crying terror.

"Zilvan, Zilvan, help me, please help me."

Zilvan touched the please button.

"Enter, Rytan."

Rytan forced a trembling hand over the scanner by using his other trembling arm to do so. He staggered through the simulated tree trunks that formed the entry portal. Axel recorded the scan, preserving the date, time, and identity of the citizen making it.

"Zilvan, Zilvan, ask them for mercy for me. Make them stop the pain. Please make them stop the pain."

He began crying as Zilvan helped him onto the M-couch. The crying continued as his body jumped into erratic patterns of agony, even when he was lying on his back atop perfect support.

"Devils!" hissed Zilvan, fist pounding a palm as he paced. He stopped to stare at his friend's suffering.

"Devils!" he yelled. "Insane with your power! You have forgotten that you are animals, too, common herd animals who eat and shit and fuck and die. You have no right to stop him from eating flesh, even if it is raw."

"Give me a sedative," he ordered the console, "and shut off the sound."

Nothing happened when he reached towards the console.

"Please."

The door opened to reveal a red glass with blue liquid. The hub went totally silent. He fed the liquid to Rytan slowly, cradling his head in one arm.

"Drink this, my friend, my ally. We will fight together. We will make them pay. Oh, how we'll make them pay."

Zilvan rocked his friend's head until the sobbing stopped and sleep claimed him.

CHAPTER 4

The Inn of Joy was Hydilla's own creation. In it, she practiced and taught the art of dance to students from all levels. Because there was no law on Logos based on genital morality, she could, and did, carry her specialties to heights that made her famous throughout the space city. Tonight, from her Trilogy of Primitive Rites, she was to do the Dance of Submission.

The audience was packed with seven, eight, and even a few nine-foot-tall Logotians. Interspersed in the crowds, almost like children, the four, five, and six-foot tall Level Niners struggled to see around those who blocked the nearest screen. Their efforts, successful or not, were completely ignored.

Holographic images were transferred to viewing areas throughout the space city. Sound patterns, from low, thundering rumbles, to barely audible highs, played on the nervous systems of the audience, stimulating their expectations. The lights dimmed, and Hydilla, nude and barefoot, strutted onto the stage.

In her left hand was a long diaphanous ribbon in electric green; in her right hand was one of brilliant orange. She paraded about the stage, using the veils to both reveal and conceal. Her manner was haughty and arrogant, yet inviting and daring. As her body moved, it played its own accompaniment by altering the soundless waves of energy flowing across the stage.

She stood spraddle-legged and erect. She began twirling the ribbons by their handles, creating patterns in the air that seemed to be made out of music – slowly at first, then increasing in speed and complexity until the images were three-dimensional and the mind raced to find meaning in the patterns. Finally, the tips of the scarves dipped down to touch her body, flicking each nipple, racing upward on her inner thighs, snaking across her vulva, crossing over the gentle mound of her belly. Her music was dotted with little grunts and moans, accenting the complicated melodic structures. The audio system picked up every sigh and delivered them evenly to all twelve levels of Logos. Even the brush of the fabric against her pubic hair was clearly heard.

"I am limbic woman," she breathed. "I lust and I hunger."

She bent backward until her hair touched the stage. As her arms went back to support her, the veils failed to protect her from observations by thousands of eyes. She moved rhythmically back-and-forth to the edges of the stage, up and down, side-to-side, twisting, turning, presenting every possible view of every part of her anatomy, setting up a driving tempo that captured all of the people of Logos in a matching submission to her beat. The segment ended when she dropped to her knees and bowed her head to the floor.

The music stopped. No sound intruded on the sudden silence for several seconds. Then she rose and spun to a new stage position.

Standing stock still, breathing rapidly, she thrust her firm breasts slightly forward, first one, then the other, producing alternating chords that worked themselves into a pulsing rhythm which continued even after she stopped. Then, amid a flurry of veils, she danced against an unseen partner. She snarled, bit, and wrestled, approached and ran away. The shadowless light of the stage became cluttered with round columns of dark shadows into which she ran and hid.

"Fill me up," she spoke from each shadow. Here, it was a demand, there, a plea, elsewhere, a prayer. From the last shadow, it was a scream.

The audience went wild, yelling, screaming, and whistling.

The lights went back to normal, but Hydilla was not in sight. The back curtain slowly opened to reveal her, still nude, but without the veils. Seven nude men, masked and cowled, surrounded her. The stage moved forward until all were transported to full view. She began moving her hips from side-to-side, slowly, then, building to the rhythm of her own rapidly beating heart, magnified to drum beats.

"We choose," she breathed. "We women choose. We make the men prove their worthiness, and then we choose."

She turned to the man nearest her. Her hips added a forward motion.

"Run for me. Run 'til I know you are fit. Run. Run. Run."

He ran, weaving his way among the others until another dancer tripped him, and he fell at her feet.

"Go," she ordered.

A column of shadow appeared and he crawled off into it. When it vanished, he, too, was gone. She whirled to another.

"Sing for me. Sing until your song fills me up. Sing until my life is yours. Sing. Sing. Sing."

He began singing and, as he sang, she danced to others.

"Play for me, earn for me, think for me, build for me," until all were active.

One by one, she danced in front of each man, sending each one into banishment by commanding, "Go!"

The last man had been ordered, "Lust for me. Lust that I will know you are mine forever. Lust. Lust. Lust." She bent over backward before him, this time without supporting herself on her arms. They were stretched out to surround him. Her body vibrated.

"Go!" she commanded.

He ran towards the last remaining shadow, then turned back to look at her.

"I lust for you," he growled.

He began a dance that quickly built up to her own level of frenzy and ended in penetration. As he entered her, she collapsed with him to the floor.

"Go," she whispered.

CHAPTER 5

Rytan, still suffering pain, tried to tell his story the next morning.

"I like the taste of blood, Zil, all blood. The taste of rabbit blood is different from squirrel blood. The blood of birds and fish, all different."

"That's weird," said Zilvan

"I know." He moaned. "Oh, Zilvan, it hurts so bad. They made me eat three raw mice. As soon as I bit into the first one, the pain gushed into my throat from its severed artery. I can still feel it. It's designed to make me hate the taste of blood. I can still feel it."

He began choking and gagging. Zilvan's face paled. "Don't go on, Ry. Wait 'til you're better."

"I have to talk. I can conquer it if I can talk. I stood it at first. I thought I could learn to like it. I had to eat each mouse in three bites. I could take as long as I liked but, until the ordeal was completed, I would not be released, even if it took a hundred years."

"Rytan, I..."

"Don't interrupt!"

Zilvan settled down to listen as his friend visibly controlled himself.

"I vowed to myself that it wouldn't take a hundred minutes. It took me five hours. No one else has ever gotten out of aversion therapy so fast. There were people there for fifteen years. They had their years scratched into their cubicles. One had written, 'please', another, 'mercy', another just 'no'.

"I got to rest between mice. I needed to. Cutting my flesh was nothing compared to this. Oh, no. Nothing.

"I figured they wanted me to take long rests so the next phase would be worse from fear. I was determined to cheat them of their goal. It was worse, all right, but not from fear. It was slow-motion agony. It was like time slowed down, like each bite took an hour and there was no taste of blood or meat. I tasted only pain, smelled only pain, heard only pain. My eyeballs were purified pain and my skin hurt from the inside so bad that I tried to tear open my belly to free the pain.

"They've got it rigged so you can't pass out, so there was no rest in the rest period, only abated agony. My mind still worked, though. Some tiny little piece of my mind knew that I would make it. 'Six-ninths of the way through,' I told myself. I used every trick I knew about handling pain. 'There is an end to it,' I promised myself. Pain past is pain forgotten.

"They should have stopped after two and left well-enough alone. I was ready to swear off raw flesh and anything else they wanted. But they still made me eat the last mouse. Zilvan, I never want to eat raw flesh again."

He sobbed. Zilvan hugged the crying face to his chest until Rytan sat up again with renewed composure.

"I don't know what I'm going to do. I'm trapped inside a body that demands flesh and blood, but with a mind tortured into denying it. My mind can't even approach the idea any more. It's like it's been sealed off in spite of my resistance. My thoughts just bounce off or detour around visualizing eating meat. And I still suffer.

"The blood and the flesh, they cleanse me in some way. Afterwards was always like being healed. Everything was renewed: confidence, energy, spirit. It cost no one anything. The animals never suffered. They were either unconscious or newly dead when I ate them. The Garden, the Archons, the Logotians - nothing and no one were harmed by what I did. I didn't even do it very often. You know that."

Zilvan nodded agreement.

"The third mouse began with hell as the first bite and went from there, to something never before described. It can't be described. But that same tiny part of me held on.

"All thought of flesh was gone. 'You will not have my will; you will not have my will.' That's all I could manage. I heard myself mumbling it over and over. I was still mumbling it when I took the third bite."

Rytan convulsed and screamed simultaneously.

"Slip your mind away from it, Rytan. Let it go. You are safe here. The pain will go away. You will forget."

Rytan relaxed into a stupor. Zilvan unclenched his friend's fists and stroked his face with gentle palms.

"We'll pay them back, Rytan. You and me and Hydie. We'll make them pay."

Rytan seemed more fully recovered when he roused from his stupor.

"I'm hungry," he announced.

Zilvan went to a covered object, moved it out from the wall and took the cover off.

"Behold my ancient fire oven! I made it myself with dirt from the Garden and plans from a primitive Earth recipe...only I added my own touches. See how the chimney curves around? That condenses the smoke so that Axel doesn't get alerted to combustion. Not even the aroma escapes, so I have a special smelling chamber. See here? When the meat is cooking, you can smell it to your heart's content."

"I'm whelmed, Zilvan. And you wanted to talk to me about keeping secrets."

"It doesn't matter now. We both know each other's secrets. I don't think any the less of you for it. In fact, I feel even closer."

"You're right. It doesn't matter. What does matter is that you're the only person on Logos that I feel safe in coming to."

"Thanks, Rytan. I love you, too. Look, I have two rabbits I can fix for us." He looked at him sharply. "Would you like yours raw?"

Rytan went immediately into a spasm. Zilvan reached for him.

"No! Leave me alone. I have to beat this thing. Just give me a minute."

While his friend recovered, Zilvan opened another container. From it, he took out bits of grass, twigs, and two chunks of wood. He opened the door of his oven, lit a piece of grass with a sparker, fed the twigs to the flame slowly, and then laid the chunks down in the fire. When they were fully ablaze, he closed the door, leaving the draft hole at the base as the only opening. He turned to face Rytan, now fully recovered from his attack.

"I'll cook them for us," he said. "It will relieve your hunger."

"I saw it with my own eyes, and I still don't believe it. Axel is virtually alive with thousands of sensors everywhere and you can get away with fire. Are you smart, Zilvan, or just lucky?"

Zilvan's face turned serious. "I'm smart. I figured out every step. Logotians seem to think that Axel is all-powerful. You probably do, too."

Rytan nodded in agreement.

"Well, it isn't. Axel has built-in levels of deviation tolerance. I found it out by accident when I failed to recycle a fox's body. It lay for three days in the dark part of the Garden. Axel had to know it was missing because it had not eaten nor occupied its den. Yet, there was no signal, no alarm.

"I decided to steal its food allotment. I stored the food until there was another litter. Then, instead of recycling the surplus pups, I kept one. I recycled the dead fox by adding a bone here and there with other dead animals. Axel never knew the difference."

"You're right, Zilvan. You're smarter than I ever gave you credit for. As a supervisory technician, I know of the deviation tolerance, but I never dreamed that anyone could manipulate it like that...least of all, you."

Rytan grinned his animal-like snarl at seeing the discomfort on Zilvan's face.

"Don't be angry, Zil. I just meant that you've always been above suspicion, not that I thought you were dumb. How did you make the fire work?"

"The same way. According to instructions, every leaf, every blade of grass, every stick had to be accounted for. The totals of the weight volumes had to be in balance. I began stealing a tiny bit at a time. I used mud from the Garden's lake to build the fire chamber. It's designed to let no fumes escape. Once the smoke cools, I recycle the solid waste with other things. I've been cooking my own meat for over a year now."

"Amazing," said Rytan. "Can we eat now? I'm enormously hungry."

"Not yet. The smoke has to cool first. That's the only flaw in my plan; the meat is almost cold by the time we get to eat it. Why don't you relax here and wait until I get through with my chores? My star is on guest status so you can order what you want from Axel. I'll be back in two hours. Is that all right?"

"That's great, Zil. I owe you a lot."

"Well, then, while you're waiting, think about this." Zilvan's face became quite serious and his body tensed. "I want the supervisor access codes to Axel. I've decided to make Logos return to Earth, and I want to use Axel to do it."

Rytan's mouth opened in amazement as he stared in shocked silence at his friend.

"Don't answer now. We can talk about it later," said Zilvan.

Rytan's mouth was still open as Zilvan exited his star.

CHAPTER 6

Rytan and Zilvan were enjoying their illegal sustenance when the call went out from the Archons to all citizens via their wrist slaves. Every activity of the communicators was suspended for the Command-level message.

"Attention, attention, attention. This is Egis, Archon of Level Five. Most of you already know that we have been hit by something from outer space. What you do not know is that all of us are in imminent danger of death. The object has lodged itself with such proximity to the virtual heart of Axel that, should it penetrate further, destruction is assured.

"We have examined all possibilities for its removal. There is no way for removal to be accomplished without the aid of a human being. I'm sorry to say that no ordinary Logotian can do the job because of the weakening of our bone structures. Therefore, I am appealing for volunteers from Level Nine. We need someone who is short, muscular, brave, and smart. If you are such a one, or if you know of such a one, please report immediately to the Council Chambers. End of transmission."

"It sounds like they have you in mind, Zil," said Rytan.

"Not me. I wouldn't lift a finger to help Logos."

"You wouldn't just be saving Logos, you'd be saving all of the lives on Logos -including your own."

Zilvan stopped chewing on a rabbit leg. "It can't be that serious."

"Yes, it is. Before I went to rehab, I was briefed on the impact. Something, we don't know what, broke through the shields and lodged just above Axel's memory complex. If the object goes five feet further, we're all dead."

"That's what one of the repair chiefs told Hydie and me. We'd just gotten out of the Space Center before the missile broke through."

"What in the holy name of fire were you doing in the Space Center?"

"I'd just come back from trying to destroy some external gauges. Hydie was standing watch for me."

Rytan laughed. "Talk about a fool's errand! Those gauges are designed to resist meteorite impacts. It's a funny picture. You might as well try to bend steel with your tongue."

"Yeah, well, I had to try. Don't laugh at me. I want to reach Earth so bad I'd do anything."

"You'd better volunteer, then. Somebody has to get that thing out or there'll be no one left alive."

"No, not me." Zilvan laughed. "I don't want any part of it."

"Listen to me, Zilvan. I don't want to die. The way I see it, you're the logical one for the job. There isn't another Level Niner as qualified as you. They're all sick, or maimed, or crazy or just plain dumb. I'll tell you something else. The missile went through one of the Command Level console rooms. With supervisor level access codes, you'll be able to learn everything."

Zilvan stopped chewing, lost in sudden thought. "You'll give me the codes?"

"Yes, Zil, I'll give you the codes if you volunteer."

Zilvan stood up and smiled. "Consider it done, my friend. What are the codes?"

Rytan smiled back. "Let's finish eating. I'll brief you. They're really quite simple to use once you know them and have access to the proper consoles. Most of the codes wouldn't be worth a damn outside of the console rooms.

"Here," said Zilvan. "You finish my rabbit. I'm too excited to eat another bite."

Rytan laughed and accepted the additional food. Between mouthfuls, he taught Zilvan what to do. As soon as the briefing was completed, Zilvan left. "I'm on my way, Rytan. Please touch out the guest status when you go. I don't want anyone else to know about my animals."

"Of course, Zilvan. Good luck!"

Zilvan pressed the entry signal outside of the Council Chambers.

"Please identify yourself," came one of the many voices of Axel.

Zilvan passed his palm above the scanning plate in front of him, placed at shoulder level for the average Logotian, but just above his head. A video screen flashed instantly on:

ZILVAN, 27539791-A

"What is your purpose here?" asked a human voice from within.

"I have come to volunteer."

The partition in back of him closed and the one in front of him opened.

"Welcome, Zilvan!" The eight Archons spoke as one.

Zilvan took off his floppy Garden cap and held it in both hands in front of him. He entered slowly, stretching his neck to stare all around the domed ceiling of the Archons' Chambers, gleaming with backlit, ever-changing panoramas of scenes from historic Earth, as were the walls.

"Thank you, sirs. I've seen holograms of the Chambers, or course, but they were nothing compared to this."

"That's kind of you to say, Zilvan," responded Tabor, who was obviously ancient, toga-clad, and holding the scepter of command. "We know of your desire to return to Earth, so we ordered these scenes for you. After your job is done, they will be made available to you for as long as you like. Come forward and relax in the magnetic couch between LeeLee and Org. We want you to be quite comfortable."

"Like a monkey in a tree," whispered LeeLee as he and Org held up their hands. In the perfect audiophonics of the Chambers, the whisper was quite clearly heard. So was Org's snort. He and LeeLee wore identical fake feather robes. She, a mere seven feet tall, had strikingly beautiful features. Org could easily have been her father.

Zilvan shuffled. "No thank you, sirs. I wouldn't feel right about that. I'm from Level Nine, you know."

"We know, Zilvan. There's nothing wrong with being from Level Nine."

"No, sir. Then why don't we have our own Archon?"

Tabor's voice turned sharp. "This is not the proper time for such questions. We need your help, not your politics. All of Logos is in danger of total destruction. You wouldn't want to see that happen, would you?"

"I might, sirs. If it made Logos go back to Earth, I might. What's your problem?"

"*Our* problem, Zilvan?" said Quandar, irritation in his voice. "You live here, too."

Quandar had a fifty-year-old face - too young for an Archon, but he got it through the assistance of Axel. He was quite vain.

"I wouldn't if I didn't have to. I'd rather be back on Earth, even if it killed us. At lease I'd be recycled by nature instead of by Axel."

Org, lying on his back with his hands behind his head, glanced only once at each new development in the Chambers, then resumed studying the scenic ceiling. Now he spoke in a soft whisper to the LeeLee on his left. "Level Nine ought to be recycled, Retros and all. They're limbic barbarians, and that's all they'll ever be." The acoustics were so perfect that every syllable was clearly heard, something obviously known to all of them. Zilvan recognized it as a tactic and did not rise to the bait.

"Org," said Tabor. "We're not in privy. Please…."

"My apologies, gentlemen," interrupted Org. He rolled onto his side facing Zilvan and said, "Tell me, did you notice your fellow citizens on the way to Chambers?"

"I sure did. They sounded scared to death that you all might leave them…just like your ancestors abandoned Earth. I laughed so hard at their antics of fear that I had to stop at a relief station. The people were so nervous that I had to wait in line."

The snickers that followed broke the tension.

"Please don't go on," asked Tabor. "The situation is not what you imagine it to be. Something has struck Logos. It tore through our shields and lodged deep within Axel. It threatens to break through to the memory complex. The artificial gravity would go. So would the air systems, the waste systems, and everything else you take for granted. Not one machine would respond to your will. You spoke of bringing Logos to Earth. Would you stand outside and push it? If you would realize your dream, you must preserve its source. Without Axel, there is no Logos."

"What is it you want me to do?" asked Zilvan, apparently chastened.

"We want you to remove the meteorite."

"I'm ready. Just tell me what to do."

As Roblen briefed him on the problems and proposed solutions, Zilvan was excitedly cooperative, showing no trace of fear.

When the presentation was completed, Quandar spoke. "Perhaps he should be briefed on the danger?"

"That's true," said Tabor. "Roblen, please brief us all on the dangers he faces."

"There is no danger to Zilvan as long as he's careful and does what he's told. He will wear protective gear, be in constant communication and be continuously controlled."

"What if I make a mistake?" asked Zilvan.

"Then you could die."

Zilvan's confident grin faded to a tremulous smirk. He swallowed. "I can do as I'm told. After all, I take care of the Garden. What shall I do with the object?"

"Do with it? Do with it? Why, eat it, of course. Tabor, I ask you, is there no one else in Logos more qualified than this? Or is this Council just sending out the most expendable?"

"You're out of order, Org," snarled Roblen. He turned to Zilvan. "This is nothing that you are required to do, but I can promise you this: if you succeed, you will become one of the most admired and respected men in the history of Logos. You will be a hero, our first hero, and anything a grateful people can do for you will be done."

Zilvan gave no outward sign of understanding what Roblen was saying. "I'm ready when you are. Will this help me get into the mating cycle any sooner?"

"Such matters are not within our power, Zilvan. Axel makes all of those decisions. As keeper of the Garden, surely you can understand that. Does he not control which animals breed and which do not and when?"

Zilvan was instantly angered. "But I'm not an animal," he began. "Retros are not animals...."

"We have no time for such dialogue," interrupted Roblen. "Look."

He touched a control and a screen came alive with moving graphs that described Axel's second-by-second condition relative to its many functions. Gravity deterioration though slow, was nevertheless the most swiftly moving graph.

"At that rate of increase, out citizens will not be able to walk much longer; they'll be flying. You are a genetic throwback, Zilvan. Your bones are not elongated like ours are. We haven't your strength. If an ordinary Logotian flies into anything solid, bones break. Your body can take stress. That's why you're the man for the job. Besides, the citizens are already showing signs of panic. Watch."

He touched in a control that showed the people of Logos milling through the miles of glinty-blue corridors like ants in a display. They chattered, each demanding of the others what they knew. When no answers were heard, fear rippled through them like the movements of a snake. Children were crying. Men and women alike began shouting, "It's all over! We have nowhere to run to! Where are the Archons? Have they abandoned Logos already?"

"We have to tell them that there is hope," resumed Roblen, "and we have to tell them soon. Will you forget your personal feelings and devote yourself to the work at hand?"

Zilvan, now contrite, fussed with his cap and said, "Yes, sirs, I just want…" His voice trailed off. "Tell me what I need to know," he snapped as he took control of himself.

"Good man, Zilvan!" said Tabor.

Sounds of approval came from the other Archons. Roblen began instructions in a sharp and distinctive voice. "First of all, you'll be right in the heart of Axel. Don't touch anything you don't have to touch. Disconnect hot or smoking wires first, then the broken ones. Don't go after the object until all of that is done. Radioactivity is quite high, so we won't be able to assist you."

"Because of your anti-pain modules, right?" Zilvan was smug with his knowledge. "Radioactivity would knock out your APM's, and you'd have to feel pain just like the Retros do, right?"

"That's not important, Zilvan. You'll be in protective gear, and you'll be in constant two-way communication. As you feed us data, we'll make decisions about your next moves. Now then, is there anything you want before your start, anything at all? We want your mind clear and easy."

"I can't think of anything, unless maybe Hydie could help me suit up."

"Hydie? Do you mean your twin sister, Hydilla?"

"Yes, sir. Her number is 27539791-B."

"Very well. Will you summon her, Quandar?"

Quandar, without speaking, touched in the number at a console. She answered almost at once.

"Hydie, ho, it's Hydie here," she sang. "For fun and fantasy, you can't beat what I do, 'cause I'm the best. What can I do for you?"

"Hydilla, this is Archon Quandar. Your immediate presence is requested. Your brother is about to perform a great service for all of Logos. He wants you with him as he prepares. Will you come?"

She hesitated only a moment. Her voice became serious, but spilled out with the same eagerness as before. "Of course I'll come. What are you going to do with him? Is he in any danger? Don't you dare do anything until I get there. I'm practically there. Errr, where shall I go?"

Org groaned.

"Meet us in the antechamber to the console room on Level Five," said Quandar.

"Goodbye," she said, without further ado.

Quandar resumed his place on his magnetic couch.

"Roblen," said Tabor, "you will please take command."

"Very well. We will go now and meet Hydilla."

CHAPTER 7

Hydilla was already in the antechamber when the Archons arrived. She and Zilvan looked as much alike as a man and woman can. Her blond hair, as his did, flowed in soft waves to shoulder length. Their blemish-free skin and perfect teeth offered evidence of the quality of care attained on Logos. Both of them, however, had eyes that were set about one inch too close together. She rushed up to her brother.

"Zil, what's going on? Why are people so frightened? What do you have to do with it?"

"Aw, it's nothing. Someone threw a rock and Axel swallowed it, so I have to go in and get it out. Come on. I want you to help me to suit up."

She went with him into the gear locker that Roblen had opened.

"Please hurry," said Roblen and left them alone.

Hydilla, dressed in opaque spray-on colors of her own design, knelt at her brother's feet. She took the vial he handed her and, with its self-contained dauber, spread a trail of liquid around the cuff of the brilliantly reflective suit he had traded for the camouflage clothes he wore for his Garden duties. The liquid gave off radiance as it sealed the fabric onto his protective boots. She continued upwards on all seams until his mask was all that remained. As she worked, he told her all that he had found out about the crisis, including the flurry about returning to Earth. She laughed at that part.

"I wish I was as bold as you," she said. "I can't imagine going up against all of the Archons and right in their own Chambers at that."

He laughed, and then turned serious and whispered to her. "Hydie, listen. I've gotten a hold of the supervisor access codes. While I'm inside, I'm going to try to find out when I'm scheduled for mating."

"Oh, Zil, don't. Don't fool around with Axel. Wait, please. You'll be punished."

"What can they do to me? I've already got one of the lowest jobs on Logos. Scraping birdshit off of leaves for recycling isn't exactly fun. But, as a breeder, I'll get privileges. You'll have a nephew and our bloodline will not die with me."

"Maybe so, but I wish I had an APM right now. I'm so afraid for you that I hurt."

"I'm glad you don't have one. If anything happens to me in there, I'd rather know you were crying instead of just blinking your right eye and going on about your business. Kiss my forehead for luck, and then seal my mask."

She looked at him seriously for a moment, then broke into a grin and kissed his forehead.

"Thanks, Hydie," he grinned back as she sealed up his mask. "Let's go."

"Are you ready?" asked Roblen. He was black and wore his hair in two-feet-long dreadlocks.

Zilvan nodded, turned, and entered without hesitation into the smoky, weirdly lit, central control complex that was Axel's very heart. Sparking wires, multi-hued instrument panels, and glowing view screens played an eerie dance on the swirls of smoke briefly visible as the airlock door closed behind him.

"It's an awful mess in here," he reported. "Wires are smoking and sparking everywhere. I'm going after the big ones first."

"Thank you, Zilvan," responded Roblen. His dreadlocks snapped as he jerked his head from side to side. "Please give us a running report on anything you touch, what you see, and every move you intend to make. You have to be precise, careful, and deliberate."

"Whoo, boy! That yellow one is as big as my ankle. It's flopping around and shooting sparks as big as my…."

"Zilvan! Don't touch it!"

Roblen's warning was too late.

"Got it!" yelled Zilvan. "What shall I do now?"

"Don't do anything," snapped Roblen. "Don't even move. Any one of those sparks can kill you. This is why I wanted you to ask first before you did anything. Where do you have hold of it?"

"About a foot back from the end of the insulation. There's another foot of wire beyond that. The other end of the wire is somewhere in the left side of the compartment."

"So is the shut-off switch," answered Roblen. "Zilvan, don't move. If the wire you're holding sparks again, you're dead. I need time to think."

"Think fast, then. I'm lying on my belly. I reached into the compartment to grab the other end. Now the compartment door is trying to close on my arm. The edges are jagged. They could tear into my arm fabric."

"What does that mean?" Hydilla asked Tabor.

"If the suit tears, he will die of radiation poisoning," said Tabor without thinking. "Logos would be lost."

Hydilla began crying. Tabor turned to look at her. "Sorry," he said.

Roblen's frame was rigid with the force of his concentration. Suddenly, he spun to face Tabor. "Weightlessness!" he barked. "Tabor, we have to shut down the artificial gravity. The cable will be suspended and then Zilvan can let go, kick his way across, and shut off the power at the primary control console."

"There must be another way," protested Tabor. "To shut down gravity would only add to the people's distress. I can't allow that."

"The people are already damn near floating," said Roblen. "There may be another way, but I don't know what it is. If you do, then please assume command."

"Now, now," said Tabor. "There's no need for belligerence." He looked around at the other Archons. Every eye was fixed on him.

"Please?" said Hydilla, drying her eyes.

"There may not be another chance," said Quandar.

"When there is but one thing left to do, Tabor," said Roblen, "then it must be done, regardless of other considerations. Will you give the order, or will you relinquish command?"

With slight nods, the other Archons indicated a unanimous yes vote.

"Very well," sighed Tabor. "So shall it be."

He pulled a necklace stone from beneath his toga and inserted it into an unmarked indentation in the nearest wall. The stone began to glow bright orange.

Axel's voice said, "Archon command level. Identify yourself, please. I am wounded."

"I am Archon Tabor."

"Verified. Your command?"

"Shut down the artificial gravity on my order."

"Confirmation by two other Archons is required. I am injured."

Quandar was the first to fish out a necklace stone from his tunic, insert it into the indentation and say, "I am Archon Quandar. I confirm." Roblen followed suit immediately.

Zilvan, in seeming quiet submission to the circumstances, broke into the hubbub of the room. "Hey, Roblen, "I'm getting a little nervous down here. The compartment door has stopped moving. One of the jagged tongues of metal has caught up against another one. Trouble is, I don't think it's going to hold."

"That's good news, Zilvan. It buys us a little more time to do what we have to do. We're shutting down gravity. Then, you can let go of the cable and it will remain in place. You must then enter the main control console and deactivate the power switch. Do you understand?"

"You bet I do. Listen to this."

The sound of metal groaning against metal was clearly heard.

"Is there any way to deactivate the compartment door controls?" asked Tabor.

"Not a chance. They were designed by Axel to protect Axel. There's too much redundancy scattered in too many places."

"Hey, Archons. Can I talk to Hydie?"

"Certainly," said Tabor. "Quandar?"

Quandar motioned her to a control panel and touched a switch. In spite of the strain showing on her face, her voice was bright, as if she were about to burst into laughter.

"Hydie ho, Hydie here! What's on your mind, Champ?"

"What's going on out there?"

"Just about a thousand Logotians waiting out here with all the good thoughts in your world for you, that's all. Are you all right?"

"Just about a thousand, eh? Think maybe we could get a party going after this is over?"

"Wow, I wish you could see the grins and signals. Zil, I think you're going to have the party of your life when this is over."

"Sounds great, Hydie...oh, oh. Hey, Roblen. You'd better hurry. The door just slipped again. It stopped an inch from my biceps. If it slips again, there's nothing left to stop it except me. My arm is starting to quiver. I can't hold on much longer."

"Shutdown sequence is complete," interrupted Axel's voice. "Awaiting your command. I am not well.'

"Activate now!" ordered Tabor.

"EEEEEEEYYYYYYYAAAAAHHH!" shrieked over the loudspeakers from Zilvan's throat. The crowd shuddered as their feet left the decks in unison with the yell.

"My arm is free!"

"Quickly, Zilvan, go into the main console compartment and press the purple-and-white switch. Don't touch anything else."

A short, grinding sound, followed by a thud, came over the sound system.

"The compartment door just closed. Guess I'm pretty lucky. Thanks, Archons. I'll tell you everything from now on. I've learned my lesson. Hey! I like this no gravity! What a whee! I'm in the main control section. I've found the switch. I pressed it. It changed from striped to solid purple."

"That's fine, Zilvan. Now wait until gravity is restored," said Roblen as he nodded at Tabor.

"Reinstate gravity, Axel", yelled Tabor, hanging in the center of the room.

As gravity was restored, bodies tumbled down again to the decks. A few screams were heard as bones cracked from the impact. The screams were foreshortened, however, as the Logotians activated their Anti-Pain-Modules.

"LeeLee and Org," said Tabor, "please attend to the supervision of damage control. I think I've broken something."

The Archons rushed to his aid. Zilvan used the recovery time to his own advantage. He quickly touched in the proper access codes, then his name. A screen in front of him lit up with a message:

> ZILVAN, 27539791-A
> Genetically defective.
> Mating status: Disallowed.

He stared at the screen in disbelief. He cancelled the command, and then reentered it. The message repeated identically. Roblen's voice broke through his shock.

"Zilvan, report. Are you all right? Zilvan. Zilvan. Zilvan. Report."

"I'm here, Roblen. I'm all right. Just a little shocked, that's all."

"I understand, Zilvan. You're a brave man, but the job is not complete. Can you continue?"

"Continue? Yes, I can continue. What shall I do now?"

"You have to enter the tunnel the missile created. Follow it until you can see what it is, then describe it to us. Do not touch it. I repeat, do not touch it."

A shuddering sigh came clearly over the sound system. "All right, Roblen. All right. I'm on my way. It sure is tight in here. I feel like a sausage in a casing. There. I'm in and on my way. The tunnel seems to curve downward. I still can't see the object yet, though. There! I see it!"

"Tell us what you see, Zilvan. Describe it to us."

"It's beautiful! I've never seen anything so lovely in my life. The colors, I mean. They chase each other around inside of the rock. Funny - I'm starting to feel sleepy."

"Katamerite!" said Roblen. "Don't stare at it, Zilvan. It can hypnotize you. Drop your ultra-violet visor into place and you'll be safe."

"Done," said Zilvan. "What next?"

"You won't be able to lift it. It weighs hundreds, maybe thousands of pounds. You'll have to hook it up to an anti-gravity harness."

"Where do I get one of those?"

Roblen looked startled at the question, and hesitated before answering. "You'll have to come out to get one."

"All right."

The crowd went silent. So did the sound system, except for Zilvan's sped up breathing. Then: "I'm stuck. My suit is caught on something. I can't get out."

Tabor's face went white. His voice was crisp and hard-edged. "You have to, Zilvan. We have no one to send in after you."

"You'd better find somebody! I can feel the strain no matter if I try to move forward or backward. I'm hooked at my right hip. I can't get my hand down there."

"I'll go," said Hydie.

Roblen hesitated for only a second. "Very well," he snapped. "Get suited up. Esig, please help her. Listen, Zilvan. Your sister is coming in after you. Don't try to move. If you tear your suit, we're all dead."

"Good, Hydie, good," said Zilvan. "I've never been so scared in my life. Please hurry."

Hydilla talked to her brother reassuringly as she entered the tunnel. "Hold on, brother dear. Hydie ho, Hydie's on her way!"

Zilvan snickered. "You may be a great dancer, but your singing isn't much."

"Hush, or I'll tear your suit myself. I can see your feet now. In fact, I'm up against them. What shall I do?"

"Can you see where I'm hooked?"

"Straighten out your right leg. There. I can see now. Your suit seems to be caught in a seam in the tube. I'll use my knife to pry it open a little. Don't even wiggle. There. You're free. I'm going to back out now. Roblen sent the AG harness in with me. It's right in back of you. I'll see you outside, champ."

"I love you, Hydie."

"Forehead, Zil. Be careful, but please hurry."

The crowd cheered as she emerged. She ignored them as well as Esig's offer to help her de-suit. Zilvan's report resumed.

"There's a hollow between the crystal and the floor. If I can get the harness strap through it and around the stone, I should be able to control it. There. That's done. Now I'm sealing it onto the stone. There. All right, I'm taking the harness up from minimum power slowly. Nothing's happening. I'm at half power now. That squeaking you hear is from the straps. I may need another harness, Roblen. No. Cancel that. It just lifted. I'm at maximum power. I'm backing out now. It's coming like a dog on a leash. I'm out of the tunnel. I'm standing up. It's free. What shall I do with it now?"

It was hard to hear with everyone talking at the top of their voices. Tabor, with a voice like a thunderstorm, managed to quiet them. Roblen took over again.

"A path is clear for you to airlock 5Z. We'll jettison it from there. You've done a great job, Zilvan. You are beloved on Logos forevermore."

Tabor spoke. "You must leave now, my fellow citizens. Go and prepare a celebration. Zilvan will be ready in an hour. We must debrief him. Go quickly."

They did. The roar of their conversations dwindled into an eerie silence. Zilvan guided the harness with one hand straight across the room, into the corridor and out to the airlock. By the time he returned, the Archons were busy directing cleanup crews and Hydilla had unsuited herself. Zilvan tried to reenter Axel's inner sanctum. Tabor blocked his way.

"Sorry, Zilvan. Your job is done. Go join the others and celebrate. The Council will want to thank you tomorrow in full Chambers. Go on now. Go on and play. You've earned it."

"Wait a minute," said Zilvan sharply. "I want to talk to you. I saw a screen in there that said I'm a genetic defective; that I'm not in the mating pool. What about it?"

"Dear me," said Tabor. "That's most unfortunate. Axel handles all of that, you know. Not even the Archons can interfere. We don't know how. Goodbye. Go enjoy your party."

Tabor moved a half-step back and an opaque, soundproof door slid shut between them. Hydilla approached.

"Zil, what's the matter? You look frightening. What happened?"

"Sorry," he said. "Will you come back to the Garden with me? I have something important to talk to you about."

"I have to get ready for the party, Zil. So do you. Can't it keep? I'll talk to you tomorrow to your heart's content."

"No!" he exploded. "I told you that I wanted to look up my mating date. I did. Axel said that I'm a genetic defective and won't be allowed to breed. Some hero! I won't even be allowed to try and father a child. It's wrong. It's evil. I hate this ridiculous Logos. I hate everything about it. The way that they section us off into nine different kinds of people. Axel's constant spying, the synthetic food, the rehab torture. I promise you, Hydie, if I can find a way to do it, Logos is going back to Earth."

Hydilla waited with concern showing on her face as Zilvan paced and shouted. When he reached a lull, she spoke soothingly. "What does it matter, Zil? Plenty of others never get the chance to breed."

"Yeah. Those space freaks with their long bones and APM's. They don't care. They don't feel anything. Me, I care. I'm the last of the line. I owe it to all of my unborn descendants to keep our bloodline going. So do you. Maybe I'll just have to fertilize you." His expression changed, as if he had just realized what he'd said.

"Of course!" he said. "That's it! Hydilla, you have to have my baby, our baby. Axel can't do anything about that and neither can the Archons. What do you say?"

"I say you're tired and upset. Zil, you'd better do something to calm yourself down. I have to go now. I'm already late. You are coming to your own party, aren't you?"

"Yeah, Hydie, I'm coming. Everything's all right now. Everything's just fine."

CHAPTER 8

The lights of the stage erupted into luxurious patterns of laser light, designed, with the crescendoing sound, to carry the audience into their own peak experiences. Just before the slowly closing curtains met, Hydilla's partner left, vanishing into the smoke that hid their mating. By the time the houselights came on, Zilvan was in his chair of honor, smiling hugely.

"Zil van!" "Zil van!" "Zil van!"

The crowd's chant filled every room on every floor of Logos, led by the holocamera that fastened on every expression of his face. In perfect unison, they continued chanting, even after he swaggered his way on stage and turned to face them.

"Zil van!" "Zil van!" "Zil van!"

He changed right before their eyes. He looked at the crowd curiously at first, raising his glance briefly to different sections of the audience. Then he looked more boldly at them, cocking his head a little and grinning even wider. He raised his arms as if to embrace them. Some broke off chanting and began to yell and whistle and laugh. Soon, they were all doing it, only to abandon it, section by section, and resume their chanting. They began to clap to fill the silent spot in his name.

"Zil *clap* van!' "Zil *clap* van!" "Zil *clap* van!"

Their long upper bodies began to move in sinewy rhythms to the unwavering beat. Zilvan began shouting his own name and clapped his own hands as he first strode, then strutted, from one side of the stage to the other. It was not until he left the stage that the chanting broke into deafening cheers. As he walked up the aisle, the Logotians broke up and flowed around him like bees. LeeLee, the only female Archon, approached. The crowd parted to let her pass unhindered.

"Tell me, Zilvan," she said, "is it true that your level of Logotians have no APMs?"

He stared at her, as well he might, for she was beautiful beyond measure. Seven-feet tall, she was proportionately curved, front, back, and sides. Regal, flawless, her manner and carriage matched perfectly her poise and demeanor. A counter movement, slowly and gracefully keeping her painted body in perfect spatial balance, matched every gesture she made.

"Do you not feel pain? Have you no need for an APM?"

"Of course I feel pain. But my brain does naturally what yours does artificially. All I have to do is get excited and I don't notice pain at all. Except when it's over. Then it hurts, but that's OK. At least I know I'm alive."

"How primitive," she said. "Are all Contras like you?"

Zilvan was instantly angry. "Are we all primitives, you mean? Somewhere well below Logotians on the evolution scale? Yes! They're like me. Did you know that 98% of all discomfort on Logos is experience by us Contras?"

Before he finished speaking, Org, who had come up to stand beside LeeLee, spoke. "Yes, we know, Zilvan. And some of us think that that fact creates an unconscionable use of Logos' resources. Because we are humane, however, we are allowing Contras to die out naturally. It's the only sane way to direct our evolution and Axel handles it well. I heard you ask Tabor about your rejection from the breeding pool. It's a beautiful example of how perfectly Axel does the job."

The people nearest around stilled. APMs began clicking on. Zilvan stood up.

"Listen to this, Contras!" he yelled. "Archon Org has just admitted that Axel is programmed to breed us out of existence! I believe him. I saw my own record. It said I'm a genetic defective, a throwback, and not allowed to ever become a father."

The Logotians who heard him responded by clicking on their anti-pain modules to shield themselves from the pain in Zilvan's voice. Several Contras responded with a wave of whatever was in their hands; a glass, a piece of food, a game piece. Zilvan looked the crowd over. Every Logotian was smiling at him, but no longer chanting. The quiet was unsettling. Org smiled, too, a different kind of smile.

"Sit down, Zilvan," he said with a sneer in his voice. "Enjoy your triumph. Shall we go, LeeLee?"

"In a moment, Org. Zilvan, I have compassion for you. You are not to blame for your condition. What you are is not your fault. Fault is an archaic concept on Logos. It has no meaning for us. Try to understand. You are merely a bio-chemical-electrical generating machine. You are therefore perfect and entitled to neither blame nor credit for what you are."

She started to say more, changed her mind, and began to leave.

"Just a minute," said Zilvan. His voice was full of challenge. "I may be what you said I am, but I'm also a lot more. I'm a human being first and a Logotian second. For the good of Logos, you may have a right to tell me what to do, but you have no rights over the unborn children of my bloodline."

"Nonsense!" said Org, almost eagerly. "You exist here by our sufferance. If I had my way, you'd all be returned to Earth in parachutes. Look around you. You don't look like a Logotian and you can't talk like a Logotian. You understand only a fraction of our words and concepts. Just because you're a temporary hero, doesn't mean you have any special rights. You removed the meteorite, but so what? You only did what we programmed you to do. And now, this ridiculous celebration serves best to show how Level Niners' minds almost work. Come on, LeeLee. Let's go."

The crowd parted to let them pass. Hydilla elbowed her way through to stand where they had been. Nose to nose with Zilvan, she hissed, "You arrogant ass. You ought to be sent out to the moon-mining camps for that little stunt. Of all people to lose control with, you have to pick Org. Level Nine may as well kiss all progress goodbye."

Well-wishers pushed her aside. They crowded around him, all chattering at the same time. He broke off trying to reply to Hydilla, and turned smiling attention to his admirers.

CHAPTER 9

Hydilla palmed her way into Zilvan's star without announcement. His place was cluttered inside with cages of small animals and a miscellany of items from the Garden: pieces of wood, birds' nests, fanciful dried greenery. None of it was legitimately there, since all forms of biological materials were supposed to be recycled. Zilvan appeared from one of the arms of the pentagram, the shape of all quarters on Logos.

"Hydie! What brings you here?"

"I'm in trouble, Zil. The Council just notified me that I'm pregnant."

Zilvan froze for a moment, staring at her with his mouth open. "You're not joking? No. You're not joking. Tell me what happened."

"I was raped. Axel did a routine scan of my urine and told the Archons that I'm pregnant. The only contact I've had with a man was during my dance. In the dark shadows, it could have been anybody."

Zilvan's eye shot from right to left, then left to right. He cleared his throat. "Do you have any idea of who could have done it?"

"None. Zilvan, I'm so scared. I wish you'd never have gone after that meteorite. Then, maybe this wouldn't have happened."

"We're only afraid of what we don't know, Hydie. Look at what you do know, and you'll not be so afraid. It's a miracle to be pregnant. You're not alone. You have me. I'll take care of you. You can even move in with me if you want. You get used to the animals."

"Oh, Zilvan." She went to him and hugged him, a long, warm hug that went from head to toe. "I'm so glad I have you."

"Me, too, Hydie. If you have to be an orphan, it's nice to have someone to be one with. Now why don't you tell me what happened?"

"Well, they got me in there and started telling me about how I have to have an abortion and all that stuff. I didn't know what to say, or even what to think, so I thought, 'What would Zilvan do?' I know how much you want to keep our bloodline alive, so I thought I should do the same. So I told them I never would have an abortion. I stood up to them, Zilvan. Aren't you proud of me?"

Zilvan didn't answer right away. He seemed to be thinking over what she said. When he did reply, he chose his words carefully. "Hydie, listen to me. I'm glad you decided not to have an abortion, but you can't carry on a bloodline. Only a male can do that. Do you have any idea at all who the father is?"

"No. It's like the inside of my head is full of mud every time I try to think about it."

"I know what you mean, Hydie. Would you like some meat?"

There was no meat consumed on Logos except by Contras and that only once a year when all of their primitive celebration rites were combined into a three-day gala. No Logotian would even consider eating meat. Not only would it be cannibalism to them, but the contrast with the perfect foods that Axel created from recyclable materials made meat an unacceptable dietary item. It would be to them like eating soil to obtain vitamins.

"Meat? What are you talking about?"

"I've kept two squirrels off the list of animals. Axel allows a one-percent fluctuation in asset distribution. When they were born, I didn't report them. They're just fully-grown and at their tenderest. Shall I prepare them for a private feast? For the three of us?"

"Zilvan, I don't know. Isn't that against all the rules? What would happen if we got caught?"

His smile was immediately replaced by a scowl. "Caught? You speak as if it were wrong to eat meat. Well, it isn't. I have a right that is older and more powerful than any rules that some old men passed to control people who haven't even been born yet. I take care of the

Garden. They don't. I care for the animals, too. If I happen to eat one once in a while, it's just the animal's way of paying me back. I'll give you another surprise. I'll cook them over a real wood fire."

Fire was an unforgivable sin on Logos. All of its energy came from the sun. Power usage was strictly allotted and monitored.

"Is your mouth watering, Hydie? Mine is. Think of a nice hind leg, all flavored with real wood smoke, juicy, tender, delicious.'

She began smiling. He grinned back.

"Ah, then, so it's settled. You and our baby…your baby…no, our baby, for I will treat it as if it were really mine - will the two of you stay for supper? I'll get the squirrels ready, and then I'll build a perfect little fire."

"I feel better already, Zil. I'm so lucky to have you. I couldn't face being alone. Too much has happened for me to make sense of it all."

"Well, you just don't think about it anymore. I'll go get started. Will you be OK here, or do you want to watch me kill them?

"No, thank you!" she asserted, then, almost immediately, "How do you do it?"

Zilvan laughed. "Come on," he said. "You can see how clever your brother is. I've been doing this for a long time and never once been caught. You know why? It's because I keep my mouth shut about it. You can get away with anything as long as no one suspects. As soon as you take someone into your confidence, though, you're doomed."

"Then aren't you afraid of sharing your secret with me?"

"No. Rytan knows, too, but he's completely on our side. You and me, we're one. We're the world's closest kin. You and me and the baby. It's almost like we're really just one person. Come on. If you don't want to watch, you can close your eyes."

She followed him into an arm of his star. At the back of it, near the corridor entry, two fox squirrels played in an enclosure. As he approached, he began talking to them in a soothing and non-threatening manner.

"Tch, tch, tch. Flicker, Bicker, I want you to meet my dear sister, Hydilla. Tch, tch, tch. She and I are going to eat you tonight. Come here. That's nice, Flicker. Climb up on my sleeve."

He shut the door on Bicker, went to a compartment and pulled out a long, thin, knife. He got a bowl, sat it on the floor, and knelt behind it.

"Come on Flicker. Let's be good, now. This won't hurt a bit."

He picked Flicker off his right shoulder with his left hand, held it over the bowl, and slit its throat in one quick movement. Hydilla's fingers were over her mouth as if to stifle sound. She stared wide-eyed as the blood pumped into the basin.

"I let the blood evaporate, you see. Then, each time I legitimately recycle a squirrel, I add a little dried blood, a little hair, a bone or two. Axel never suspects. The supplies coming in match the wastes going out. Result: I get to eat meat fairly often."

He slit the squirrel's belly open from tail to chest. Its entrails spilled out like soft, coiled clay.

"These get fed to some very special Garden animals. The Logotians thought they'd bred out their carnivores. I've taught them to eat meat again. Maybe I'll show you sometime. It's fun to watch them snarl and fight over it."

He cut a slit in the hide around the squirrel's middle, stuck his middle fingers under each section and pulled the squirrel's hide off in both directions. He disconnected the hide by slicing off the paws of the creature.

"There," he said, "that's half our dinner."

His hands were bloody. The beast's body looked too human-like for consumption. Hydilla closed her eyes and turned around. "I don't want to see it anymore."

"Wait! I want you to see it! I want you to appreciate that that's exactly what your baby, our baby, would look like if you ever weakened and let them abort it."

"No, Zilvan! Don't make me look or I'll not be able to eat a bite of it. I won't let them do anything to me. I promise in the names of our unknown parents."

Zilvan smiled and lowered the squirrel's body. "Go wait for me. I'll just be a few more minutes."

She went back to the center of the star and sat quietly with head back and eyes closed waiting for him to finish. He had the two squirrels impaled on a spit when he returned. He went to a covered object, moved it out from the wall and took the cover off.

"Behold, my ancient fire-oven! I made it myself from dirt from the Garden, only I added a few touches. See how the chimney curls around? That condenses the smoke so that Axel doesn't get alerted to fire. Not even the aroma escapes, so I have a smelling port. See here? When the meat is cooking, you can put your face up to this and smell to your heart's content."

As he talked, he put the spit across the firepit. From another covered container, he took out bits of grass, twigs, and chunks of wood. He lit a piece of grass with flint and fed the twigs to it slowly, then the chunks. When they were well lit, he closed the top, leaving as the only hole a draft hole, where the fire took up oxygen. "You'll be able to smell it in a couple of minutes now."

He kept putting his face up to the smelling port. "Ah, yes. Come and smell it, Hydie. Come and smell our friends being transformed by the mystery of fire into something fit to sustain the mystery of life."

She put her face up to the port and inhaled deeply. "Ohhh," she said, "I can hardly wait. How long will it be?"

"They'll be cooked before you know it. I'll go back and clean up my mess. By the time I'm done, we'll be ready to eat."

"All right, Zil. Can I touch in some music?"

"Sure. Anything you like."

As he left, Hydilla touched in music from her dance repertoire. She began moving slowly to the piping strains. As the music picked up tempo, she began dancing. Soon, she was swirling about the room and bumped right into the oven. The top was dislodged enough to emit a single puff of smoke. She grabbed it immediately and set it right and got burned hands for her trouble. She blew on them and held them against her thighs. By the time Zilvan got back, the air system had whisked the odor away. She did not tell him of the accident.

"The squirrels ought to be done now. First, we smother the fire and wait for the smoke to condense. The meat cools down enough to handle without burning our fingers. Then we eat. Do you want any of that space stuff to go with it? Fruit? Bread?"

"No, this will be just fine."

"Hydie, I've been thinking. I want our baby to be born on Earth. Listen, when I was inside Axel, I learned more than just being out of the genetic pool. I learned some of the passwords the Archons use. I can find out stuff no Contra has ever been allowed to know. If I do things right, I might be able to interfere with Logos so that its orbit gradually decays and brings us to a soft landing on Earth."

"Zilvaan!" she protested. "First you make me feel better, and then you make me all crazy again! Give me my squirrel and shut up. You can't bring Logos down to Earth. No one can."

He handed her one squirrel straight off the spit and took the other one for himself. They sat on the floor facing each other and began eating.

"Sure I can! I can get access to the right lockers and get into the right space gear. Outside, I can damage the guidance control system…not a lot…just enough to make the orbit decay."

"What would you do on Earth, dummy? Everyone knows it's radioactive down there. You wouldn't survive. I wouldn't survive, and our baby wouldn't survive. What's the sense in it?"

"Ummm, this tastes good! The sense in it is this. Up here, we're just Contras, second-class citizens. We spend our lives doing things we don't want to do for people we never even see. Down there, we can live free, like we were meant to. Logotians aren't Earth people. They'll never want to go back. They couldn't even if they wanted to. Their bones would break in natural gravity. Org himself said that they were planning a sister city to Logos to fly right beside it. The next thing, they'll build a new Logos just to house the Contras. Up here, they have the power; down there, we do. Just think, Hydie:

you, me, the baby. We could be the start of a brand-new Earth. Doesn't that excite you?"

"Can I have some water, please? To be honest, part of me is screaming no, but part of me is fascinated."

He got up to get her some water. Just as he reached for the cup, his entry opened to admit five firemen. Each rushed to a different arm of the pod. In that brief interval, Zilvan grabbed the carcass out of Hydilla's hand and threw it and his own into a small box with a cover on it. The firemen quickly reassembled into the hub of the star.

"Have either of you created smoke in some way?" asked the nine-foot-tall, head fireman.

"Not me," said Hydilla with great sincerity.

"Me, neither," said Zilvan. "I know about the fire mandate. I wouldn't violate an important rule like that."

Though both were pictures of innocence, the fireguard was unconvinced. "I see. There was a strange odor in the air when we entered this star. What might that have been?"

"Ah, we were trying a new sensory stimulation for my sister's dance shows. You must have mistaken that for smoke."

"Axel doesn't make mistakes about smoke. What are you doing there, miss? What's the matter with your hand?"

She had unconsciously blown on it and held it against her thigh. "Nothing."

"Let me see. That looks like a burn, miss. Where did you get it?"

Her eyes strayed to Zilvan's oven. Without letting go of her wrist, he told his men to check it out. It was still warm enough in the ashes that a wisp of smoke went up from them when they were stirred. They gassed the oven immediately, and then set about examining it in detail.

"Please let me go," said Hydilla.

Instead, he looked again at her hand. He lifted her fingers to his nose and smelled them. His face got quite stern. "Search everything," he ordered.

They found the remains of the squirrels almost at once. Yet, they continued to search until everything openable had been opened and everything that was not had been cut, shattered, or disassembled.

"Both of you are under arrest," said the head fireman. "Be ready to appear before the Council within the hour."

CHAPTER 10

Zilvan showed no signs of remorse as he stood before the Council.

"Egis," said Tabor, "please refresh Council's awareness of the Fire Mandate…briefly.

"Archons," he began, "because a Contra is involved, I shall translate the Fire Mandate into language appropriate to his ability to understand. I realize that this imposes an additional burden, for it is equally as difficult for those who understand more to understand less, as it is for those who understand less to understand more. Bearing in mind the seriousness of the incident, I await your objection."

No one spoke a word. Zilvan and Hydilla stood together at the open end of an inclined V. Tabor sat at the elevated tip.

"Very well. The Mandate evolved from a prohibition against fire, from a time when materials on Logos were flammable. Since there no longer is anything on Logos, except the Garden, made of flammable materials, only the Garden is subject to the law. Originally, lives were at stake when violations were made. Today, only machinery is vulnerable." Egis, only seven feet tall, looked closely at each Archon, his staring eyes demanding contact with their eyes. Egis was old, the historian and chief interpreter of the rules.

"What an odd way of stating it, Egis," said Roblen. "Do you hold a prejudice in this matter?"

"No, Roblen, I do not. I meant only to focus on the damage the accused might have done."

"Well, you've certainly done that," said LeeLee. "I'm not sure that anything has been done that deserves this kind of attention."

LeeLee looked at the twins as the twins looked at each other. Both of them moved at the same time so that their shoulders met.

They seemed to have reassured each other in some manner. For the first time, instead of looking at the floor or the three-dimensional representations of historical Earth, they looked at the speaker. LeeLee smiled at them. They smiled back. Their smiles faded quickly, however, as Org spoke. His body was narrow, even for a Logotian, and his nose, chin, and forehead all worked together to form a wedge. He had never been known to smile, not even as a child.

"LeeLee, I am vexed by the continuing exercise of your sentimentality. I find it obnoxious at best, but here in Chambers, I find it particularly objectionable. May I remind you that it is your sworn duty to render judgments in controversial matters in favor of the betterment of the people? The offense and the punishment are clearly marked out in the Fire Mandate. I do not know which of these twins started the fire, but I surely expect Council to behave in an exemplary manner."

"Honorable Archons," said LeeLee, "if Hydilla started the fire, her punishment must be delayed until after the termination of her pregnancy under the Logotian Law of Innocence."

Hydilla and Zilvan looked at each other briefly. Hydilla spoke out in a clear voice, "I lit the fire. Let Zilvan go."

"Really?" said Roblen in disbelief. "Perhaps you will tell us how you lit it."

"I got some grass, and bark, and wood and lit it with sparks."

"Indeed," said Roblen. "What did you use to make sparks?"

Her confusion was obvious. She made no reply.

"I see," said Roblen. "Thank you, Hydilla, for telling us how it was done. Since it is apparent that you are lying, Zilvan must therefore be guilty. Zilvan, will you admit to it?"

Zilvan sidled a step away from Hydilla and looked at her as he spoke. "Hydilla had nothing to do with it. Let her go. It was all my doing."

"Let's let her go," said LeeLee. "In spite of how bold her words sound, the poor thing is trembling."

"She is also guilty of eating meat," said Org in the bored manner of reminding a child of its lesson.

"Accused, Org," said Tabor in his commanding bass.

"My apologies," said Org.

"Are you guilty then of eating meat, Hydilla?" asked Roblen.

She looked at Zilvan and did not answer.

"I see," said Roblen. "Then Zilvan is again the guilty one."

"If he is guilty, then I am guilty, too," said Hydilla.

"My, my," said Org. "What a charming manifestation of limbic loyalty. An atavistic act of altruism. Incredible. Especially when you consider the barbarous act of cannibalism they have perpetrated. May I tell them, Tabor, of the Incident of the Visitor?"

"If there is no objection...?" said Tabor. "Proceed."

Org's voice was raspy, as if the words were being drawn over shattered plastic.

"We were not always alone in the sky, Hydilla and Zilvan. Many generations ago, before we learned to survive as we do, creatures visited us. They came in a cylindrical spaceship, docked, and came aboard. They were intelligent but didn't seem to be so. They reacted to our environment like animals in a strange place. They sniffed with their long noses, peered with huge, black eyes, listened with ears that seemed to rotate on swivels, and licked at almost everything that presented itself, including us.

"They made no sounds at all. The Archons of that day, unfortunately not nearly as advanced as we are, insisted in babbling on in Earth languages. We never found out if they understood us. By the time they got to Level Nine, the Archons had deserted them to figure out ways of getting them off Logos immediately. The aliens seemed to be eating each other's waste.

"They really weren't. They had food storage pouches where we used to have tails. The fed each other to quiet their overstimulated senses. But, when the Contras saw them doing that, they were totally revolted. They decided that since the visitors looked like animals and behaved like animals, they must be animals. So they ate them.

"It was many decades later before we were able to decipher the equipment on their ship. That's how Roblen knew that the meteorite was kateremite. That's how we learned much of what we know that makes Logos successful...and Axel possible.

"We were never visited again. It's as if we have been put off limits. Or, perhaps, we've been designated as a sanctuary for cannibals. At any rate, every Archon since has regretted what happened and vowed never to let it happen again. It also serves us well as a constant reminder of what you Contras really are."

The Chambers fell into quietness when he stopped speaking. Egis broke the silence. "Eating flesh is an unauthorized use of natural resources, nothing more. The Archons, themselves, have authorized its consumption on the Contras' High Days. More than a few Logotians have tasted flesh at that time."

"Nevertheless," said Roblen, "it is a violation of law and must be dealt with as such. As for the lack of flammable material, be advised that most of our plastic will melt. It will give off dangerous fumes in the process. However, since reconstruction for Hydilla is out of the question at this time, perhaps action should also be postponed for Zilvan."

"If there is no objection..." said Tabor.

"One moment," said Org. "Zilvan is singularly responsible for that fire. I insist that he be brought to account for that."

Tabor, his face grim with displeasure, ordered that Hydilla be released and Zilvan detained. "Hydilla!" he thundered, "you will present yourself to the pre-natal complex. Until the termination of your pregnancy, you will be treated as any other mother. The Inn of Joy will be closed to you. All of your activities will be guided by the Clinic. Do you understand?"

She was trembling but her voice was clear. "How can I trust you? You could have Axel put something in my food."

"They will not!" said LeeLee. "You are a mother now and protected by the very law that you and Zilvan scorn. I offer you my own mantle of protection. Archons, please excuse Hydilla and me from the balance of this meeting."

"If there is no objection...?" said Tabor. "Proceed."

"What's going to happen to Zilvan, Archon LeeLee?" asked Hydilla as soon as they were outside of the chambers.

'Well, my dear, the Reconstruction Room was designed by Axel to solve the problem of what to do with repetitive sinners. To solve it, Axel chose associative aversion conditioning. Pain is the conditioner. In the room, the candidate is subjected to silent waves of an energy spectrum that surges through the body until no nerve is left untouched. Tiny thorns of pain bubble their way through veins and arteries, lodge in capillaries, and congest at every joint until movements meant to ease the anguish become themselves a source of agony. All they can do is lie there and cry, once the screams are exhausted. Awareness and consciousness are left to function without inhibition. The sin that brings the pain is sharply in focus the entire time.

"Zilvan will be required to light three fires on three separate days. It can take him as long as he likes; three weeks, three months, three years, whatever. Once the conditioner has worked its magic, he will be unable to light another fire...ever."

"Will I have to go through that, too? After my baby is born?"

"No, Hydilla. You will merely be retrained. Eating meat does not harm anyone."

"Setting the fire didn't harm anyone, either."

Hydilla suddenly stepped in front of LeeLee and craned her neck to look up at her. "Is there nothing you can do to help him? Nothing at all?"

"If he were the father of your child, there might be a chance. Fathers have the right of community will. They can demand a vote that could set them free."

"Zilvan is willing to act as the father of my child, and I want him to. We're all that each of us ever had."

"You can tell them, Hydilla. I cannot. Do you wish to try?"

"Please."

Zilvan still stood as he had when they left. Roblen was questioning him about the mathematics of asset distribution that permitted him to gather the materials for a fire.

"Excuse me, fellow Archons. Hydilla wishes to claim fatherhood rights for Zilvan. She says they have both agreed to this role. She further wishes him to have a Vote."

Org answered at once, "You've been very busy in such a few moments, LeeLee. I do not understand your special interest in this matter, but you can rest assured that I'll find out."

"I assure the Council that I have no part in formulating the ideas of this pair. I act only as a representative who can interpret them for the moment. Fairness is my only concern."

"Very well, then," said Tabor. He turned to Zilvan, towering over him like a giant, unhappy, father figure. "Do you understand what LeeLee and Hydilla are saying? If you become the father figure, there are certain responsibilities you must uphold. There are also certain rights, among which is the right to majority will, the Vote. If the people so decide, you may escape reconstruction based on their assessment that you would never perform such an act again. Do you accept fatherhood?"

Zilvan smiled up at the figures semi-surrounding him. "Yes, sirs!" he said eagerly, already anticipating escape from punishment.

"Do you wish for a Vote?"

"Yes, sirs!"

"Very well," said Tabor. "Will you proceed, Quandar?"

Quandar touched in a Vote call. The electronic slaves, which every person on Logos was required to have within reaching distance at all times, all turned on at once. Quandar explained the problem, and then asked if Zilvan might be exempt from reconstruction. All of the people of Logos pushed the zero or one button on their slaves at approximately the same time. Axel balanced each zero and one as obliterated pairs. When there were more zeros than ones, the surplus votes were held until they could be paired, then obliterated. When all voting had ceased, the pool of either zeros or ones voted again. The process went on until only one voter was left unpaired. No one ever knew who it was, but it was that voter's lot to decide the issue. In Zilvan's case, the final vote was zero. He was to receive no relief.

CHAPTER 11

"Zilvan," thundered Tabor in his huge voice, "you will be taken to the reconstruction area forthwith. Upon your successful completion, you will be returned here for further assessment."

Zilvan just stood there, rigid, with his fists clenched. He was working hard to hold back his temper. He seemed so small, so helpless.

"No!" yelled Hydilla. "He didn't do anything that I didn't go along with. What you are doing is wrong. Zilvan has hurt no one; neither have I."

"Did you light the fire, Hydilla?" asked Quandar.

"No, I didn't, but I would have, and I will, if you fix Zilvan so that he can't anymore. And your stupid Vote isn't fair, either. You can't allow some person who doesn't even know some other person to decide about that person's life."

"LeeLee," asked Org, "would you escort her out again? Her case has been decided."

"No!" said Hydilla. "I won't go!"

"Archon Tabor, has the Council got no more pressing matters to attend to than this?"

"You shut up!" yelled Hydilla. "You've been degrading us ever since Zilvan became a hero. What's the matter? Can't you stand a Level Niner doing what no Logotian could ever do? If it weren't for him, your stupid mandates wouldn't mean a thing because Logos wouldn't even exist."

"She has a point," said Roblen.

"She has no point at all," said Org. "If those who serve Logos well are to be rewarded outside of the law, then we as Archons ought to have no restrictions on what we do for ourselves."

"Your point, Org," growled Tabor. "Hydilla, you are excused. Please go with her, LeeLee."

Zilvan's trance seemed to be broken. He turned to look at Hydilla. "Thanks, Hydie. Go now and don't make me worry about you. OK?" He turned back to the Archons. "Do your worst. You will not break me. I am Zilvan."

A Senior Protector came to lead him away. On his way, Zilvan sang, "Hydie hi, Hydie ho. You can relax now. Your brother has everything under control."

"Take care of yourself," she yelled as he left. "Don't give them any reason to hurt you."

"No reason. That's good. No reason."

"Well," said Org, "this has been an interesting interlude. Now can we get down to the business of directing the growth of Logos and its citizens? We have to devise a way of protecting Logos from missiles like Katamerite. We must also ratify the plans for a second Logos to tether to us. Roblen, you will guide us. Please."

CHAPTER 12

Zilvan was a broken man when he emerged from reconstruction. No one greeted him anymore. His hero support vanished. Only Hydilla and Rytan were there for him, but that was enough.

All three of them were in Rytan's star.

"Zylvan, I'll give you the codes you need," said Rytan, "but they won't be enough. The system was devised early in our development. It's been overwritten so many times, it's virtually unrecognizable. Its existence was the first program developed. It was to return Logos to Earth safely. But it had to be made to happen.

"So the founders built a gravity well, lined with specialized mirrors. A knotted nylon rope was the only access. It was guarded by rays so powerful they would vaporize anything that crossed an invisible barrier."

Hydilla visited his star the same evening of his release. She revealed that the Archons were insisting upon an abortion. Zilvan, afraid of chemical interference by Axel, hid her in the Garden, freeing her from it. In the last week of her pregnancy, he decided to die in an effort to reach the antique fuse.

At the well of power, he lowered himself inch-by-inch into it. In the mirror walls, he watched himself, beginning with his toes, vanish into painless disintegration. He reached the switch. He was gone from the waist down. The fuse resisted his efforts. His grip weakened. Rytan, from above, yelled at him to turn it the other way. He did. Logos shuddered. He fought to hold on. Suddenly, he heard Axel scream. He grinned, let go, and fell, laughing, into oblivion.

Logos had just enough power left to affect a relatively soft landing. Its crumpling outer structure absorbed most of the landing shock. As the dust settled, total silence prevailed. Earthlings, by ones and twos, gathered to stare. Hydilla was the first to exit, carrying with her the newborn baby. The baby's cry was the first sound to break the silence.

The End

The Big Lonely

Heh Heh Hooley awoke slowly, the familiar hangover pounding his temple like his arteries wanted to bust through. He looked through the hole in the roof first, seeing a low, gray sky. Then, he looked towards the bottom of his sleeping bag and saw the lower half covered with three or four inches of snow. He looked over at his friend's bag and saw the same thing.

"Hey! Wake up, Smitty! It's done snowed a bunch!"

Smitty didn't move. Heh Heh crawled out of his sack and put on his featherweight hunting boots, his proudest possession. He stood up and looked around. This was his home, his and Smitty's. It was a brick cubicle, about ten by ten. During World War II, it was a pump station, supplying water from the Mississippi River to a Minneapolis factory long since defunct. Now it was a home for the homeless, minus half its roof. The covered corner was where they built their fires for warmth and cooking. He dug his foot into Smitty's bag at about the middle and realized at once from the stiffness that Smitty was dead.

"Well, I'll be damned," he said.

He unzipped Smitty's bag and laid it open. He went through every pocket on the dead man, and retrieved a sack of Bull Durham and some Zig Zag cigarette papers. Then he undressed the man. Once naked, he stripped himself, and put on the dead man's underwear.

"You won't be needin' these Damarts no more," he sighed. "It's hot enough where you're goin'."

He put his own underwear onto the body and dressed both of them as swiftly as he could. The cold was biting.

Smitty was so stiff that dressing him was not an easy job. Once done, he took the label off of a soup can and wrote on it with a stub of pencil:

"This here's Rex Smithson from Arkansas. He was baptized once so hes a cristian man and wants a cristian burial."

He folded the label and put it in Smitty's breast pocket. He went to the door, connected only by its bottom hinge, and pushed it open against the drift outside. Then he took Smitty's bag by the bottom and dragged it down to a spot on the river where an overhanging bank formed a hollow.

He tugged the body into the hollow, went back to his home for a piece of board, and used it to shovel snow over the sleeping bag until it was completely buried. He took off his Russian-style hat and prayed: "Dear Jesus, you took him while he was drunk and asleep.

Thank you for your mercy. Let it be the same with me. Heh, heh, heh, heh, heh."

He paused at his home long enough to throw the board back in and headed to the mission for a hot meal and coffee. He stayed there as long as he could before starting out to beg enough money for a bottle of wine to ease his headache, and to insure both a day's forgetfulness, and a night's sleep.

He usually begged outside the mall, but the weather was so poor and the wind so blustery that he decided it wouldn't be worth it. Instead, he headed for a nearby street where the drug people hung out. Maybe one of them, as some had in the past, would favor him. He tramped the street for three hours, grooving a path in the unshoveled sidewalks. Not a soul came around. He went back to the mission for another meal.

Afterwards, he tried the mall, but no one would give him a dime. He returned to the pusher's street. This time, he got lucky. A tall, skinny young man appeared and stopped at Heh Heh's plea. Heh Heh decided to go for broke. "Can you spare me a dollar?"

"Hell, man, I'll do better than that," he practically crowed. "You know what I did? I hit a home that some rich bastard lives in. I had to cut off the old lady's ear to make him open the safe. I'm loaded, man – in more ways than one, if you know what I mean. Man, I'm really floating. You look like a little bug to me. Sure, I'll give you a dollar, but you have to tell me your name first."

"Heh Heh."

"Heh Heh! What the hell kind of name's that?"

"It's the way I laugh that gave it to me."

"Well, Heh Heh, here's your dollar. No! Wait a minute! I got a better idea. Tell you what, here's a quarter from that rich bastard's coin collection. I figure it's got to be worth a lot more. Here, you take it. Good luck to you, man."

The young man took off down the sidewalk, kicking at mounds of snow and giggling as he went. Heh Heh headed straight for the liquor store.

"Whatta you want?" asked the clerk.

Heh Heh went for broke again. "Two fifths of Jack Daniels."

"Let's see your money."

Heh Heh laid the quarter on the counter.

"Whatta you tryin' to pull?"

"Look at it. It's a valuable coin. It used to be in a collection."

The clerk picked it up and looked at it closely. Then he pulled a pint of wine from the shelves behind him and set it on the counter. "Here," he said. "I ain't no damned coin shop. How do I know what it's worth?"

"You ain't never seen another quarter like that, that's how. Make it just one fifth of Jack Daniels."

The clerk took the pint bottle back, and put a quart of wine in its place. He took the coin and laid it on the sill of the register. "That's the best I can do, pal."

Heh Heh looked at the bottle, licked at his chapped lips, and decided to take it. The clerk slipped the wine bottle into a brown paper bag. "Git outta here," he said.

As soon as Heh Heh closed the door behind him, the clerk took some change from his right-hand pocket and rang up the sale. He looked at the quarter again and put it into his left-hand pocket. Heh Heh headed straight for the riverbank and home. Once Heh Heh was out of sight, the clerk picked up the phone.

"Frank's Coin and Investment."

"Hi Frank, it's me, Charlie. I've got another coin for you. It's a 1914 quarter with a San Francisco mint mark. It looks brand new."

"Yeah? Lemme check. OK. You've got a real winner this time. It retails for $750 in uncirculated condition."

"How much will you give me for it?"

"Three hundred dollars, if it's as good as you say it is."

"Well, Merry Christmas to me!"

"Yeah, Merry Christmas."

"I'll see you on my way to work tomorrow."

"OK, kid. Goodbye."

"Bye."

Back in his brick cubicle at home, Heh Heh got into his sleeping bag without taking any clothes off, not even his shoes, and wrapped it around his shoulders, leaving his right arm free to handle the quart of wine. He freed his left arm briefly to uncap the bottle.

"Merry Christmas, Smitty. Merry fuckin' Christmas." He held the bottle up to his lips and drank half of it without stopping.

Bridge of Stones

Junior's voice, this time, held no element of compromise. He looked at his plate instead of at me as he spoke. "As soon as 'Vina and I move into our new home, Dad, I want my rocks back."

The instant he said it, I felt a flush of anger. Why? I had everything in the world to be grateful for, sitting here at my fiancee's home, Sara Jane, complete with a loving family at a grand Thanksgiving table. *You little jerk*, I thought. *Although you are bigger and stronger than I, those are my rocks, not yours.*

"Which ones are you talking about?" I asked.

He stammered a bit as he sought to recall their names. "Well, the sagenite agate, for one. I found it, you know."

Yah, you found it, I thought. *I cut it, polished it; I learned its story. To you, it's a possession to display. To me, it's a treasure to be studied and shared with as many others as possible.* My anger flush grew. "We'll argue about it later," I said.

"What argument?" he replied. "There is no argument."

I was suddenly fighting for control of the anger that threatened my mind. *Not here. Not in front of all these people.* This is the rage I thought I'd controlled, the rage that separated father-and-son love with valleys of pain and rivers of remorse. Nine years were still not enough to conquer the old conditioned reflex of my-will-be-done.

"Well, a serious discussion then," I said.

His wife 'Vina intervened. "Would you hold the baby for a while?"

"Sure," said Junior, pleasantly, calmly.

He took the infant with practiced familiarity that made his strength a refuge to the child. *What a neat father you are*, I thought, and felt the red rage turn inwards against myself. The limbic part of me, the part that acquires, possesses, and defends, an ancient part grown strong by surviving with the fittest, pitted its strength against my powers of reason.

The economic value of the rocks was substantial. Thousands of dollars were spent in just gathering them. Thousands more were represented in their resale value. The sagenite agate was the largest known specimen of Lake Superior agate, in which fine crystal needles radiated in a fan over the full face of the stone. I'd spent many careful hours cutting and polishing to bring out the crystalline structure without destroying it.

There were many dozens more stones in the collection, some of equal value, some of greater. The eight other stones he laid claim to included three irreplaceable museum specimens. One was the world's largest specimen of thomsonite.

I'd found it while SCUBA diving in Lake Superior. I'd run out of air and was struggling to stay afloat in rough waters without dumping the stones I'd gathered. My son, standing by in a twelve-foot aluminum boat, quickly and perfectly started the engine, raised anchor, maneuvered the boat through white-capped waters, came alongside and grabbed the rocks, the SCUBA gear and me, in that order. He was thirteen years old.

As a reward, I told him that he could have all the rocks in one collection bag. I didn't know it at the time, but that bag held the world's largest specimen of thomsonite, a specimen that the Smithsonian Institution solicited for its collection. I'd held onto it and the others all this time, though I sure could have used the money. Now he was holding me to my word.

Give him the rocks. I heard the words bounce around inside my head like racquet balls. *What kind of person are you? An animal protecting a kill? You have all the rest; let him have what he wants."*

No, I won't give him those rocks. It's criminal to break up a collection like that.

Wait a minute. You're going to have to fight him about this sooner or later. Just make up your mind that you're going to keep them all, and that's that. You know you'll win. You always have.

That's the answer, all right. I'll tell him I'll leave them to him in my will. That should settle the matter, but not right now.

He sat with the baby, feeding him while his wife ate her own dinner. He seemed so gentle.

I felt content after dinner. Making such a sensible decision caused the red rage to fade into a shapeless background and let me join again in the conversation. I figured that now was as good a time as any to issue my little news bulletin. "By the way, son – my boat swamped."

For personal and financial reasons, I'd lived aboard a houseboat for the last five years, struggling to regain my health. Everything in the world that I owned was aboard the houseboat. Everything in the world that I wanted was inside of it. He looked at my face to see if I was kidding.

"How bad is it?" he asked.

"Not too bad. She's in shallow water, so everything inside is safe."

"She won't be when high water comes. I'll meet you down there tomorrow and we'll see what we can do."

"What time?"

"Noonish."

"OK."

I didn't let myself get excited about it. Too often in the past, there'd been last minute excuses or no-shows without explanation. But I went to the river anyway. The stern and starboard of the forty-two foot boat were covered with ice up to six inches thick. I'd weathered many a storm with her before, and felt proud of my ability to handle anything that came along. This time though, I was glad I hadn't been aboard.

We swung into work together like skilled dancers in a familiar routine. I felt a growing pride and sense of sameness between us that made the salvage work seem like a grand thing to be doing.

We got it all, including the rock collection. Neither of us mentioned it. We carried the contents in Junior's van back to Sara Jane's home. As we unloaded it and carried it into the basement, every aching joint and sore muscle was balmed by the pleasure of accomplishment.

"What are you doing Sunday?" he asked.

"Nothing planned."

"Good. I'll come down and fix your car."

"Super."

We'd talked about it a little during work breaks. The mechanic said it would cost about $185 to make the car safe. I said I'd need at least six months to save that much. Junior's offer seemed too good to be true. But he showed up when he said he would, and off we went for parts.

As I watched him labor for the next two hours, putting in brakes and rear-axle seals, I began to glimpse how much he loved me, in spite of all the errors and terrors my fatherhood had produced.

Suddenly, I knew what I would do. "Son, I've got a Christmas present for you that's gonna make your day."

"Oh yeah?" He looked up at me and grinned.

Ah ha! I thought. *How many times have I let him down in the past?*

He finished the job, and then we had some coffee and pie together in the house, chatting like good friends do. As soon as he left, I hurried to the basement to gather the stones that were to be his Christmas present. I intended to label each one, telling the core of its story. They were gone. Upstairs, a dozen specimens that had been put into another sack were all that remained. I felt sick.

I must have looked through the bags and boxes a dozen times, each time feeling just a little sicker. The rocks were the first item he'd packed and put aboard his van.

I should've known better. He didn't volunteer the salvage work for my benefit, but his own. And the car work – that must have been a salve for his conscience. How do I handle this one?

The ancient part of my brain screamed out for revenge. *Banish him from your life. Who needs a thief around? Who knows what he might next claim as his own and repossess under the guide of caring? Confront him, and when he admits his deed, tell him how he has confounded a gift of love, and crucify him on a cross of guilt.* I sat back and the agonizing battle began.

He is your son. If he asks for a stone, shall you give him hell? Where is your own love? What do you expect of it?

A dull, achy acceptance began setting in. *Possession is more than nine-tenths of the law; possession is power.* Such was the lesson my parenthood had taught him. He'd been a good student. We'd repossessed a lot of cars back in the good old days, when money and power were important. I'd shared the money with him, but never the power. Nevertheless, he'd learned to use and misuse it exactly the way I had. But I'd never taught him to steal.

He'll claim that repossession is not theft, but he'll not understand the exemption for the unperfected title. Nor will he consider that most of the rocks he took, he cannot possibly lay claim to. Could it be that he thinks he'd protecting the entire collection against possible claims by my fiancée? *No. That's too ridiculous to consider. Our blood bond is too strong for that.*

Blood bond. He is your son. Love him without condition or your love will never bridge the past.

Bridge. Bridge of stones. Why not?

Dear Son,

December 25th

I promised you a Christmas present that would make your day. Instead, it has made mine. I wanted to give you the entire rock collection, but it's missing and presumed stolen. Nevertheless, what's left is yours.

I've printed cards for the rocks, but the cards can't tell how I handled them when I was lonely and remembered good times, or how I stared at them when I was alone and became glad. Nor will they tell of the greater knowledge that study of the stones led me to. I hope they do as much for you.

Bridge of Stones

They are in your keeping now, and that somehow feels right and proper. You will not find the same values in them that I did, and that seems right and proper too. But there is one value in the rocks that transcends all others. They show me how much I really love you, and form a bridge for that love to travel across. And, though the rocks will eventually disappear, the love they carry never will.

Merry Christmas.

Love,

Dad

I took the rocks to him on Christmas Eve. His new home was nicely situated on the peninsula of a lake. The woods around assured me that my grandsons would grow up with plenty of access to nature. It was about time to take the oldest one out and start teaching him what I knew. Not very convenient though. Too far away. No room for extra gas in my budget.

The snow fell softly, undisturbed by wind. Huge flakes, backlit by Christmas splendor, melted away as soon as they touched my skin. He answered the doorknocker with a grin and a hug.

"Hi, Dad! Merry Christmas! Let me take that for you."

"No, no. I'll put it under the tree."

"Suit yourself. Can I take your coat?"

"Sure."

The rocks were in the box I carried in. I didn't want him to take it because the weight would give it away. The letter was in my coat pocket. I'd wait for the right time to give it to him.

As I put the box under the tree, I looked more closely at the two huge packages leaning against the wall on either side of the tree. They were each the size of four-by-eight sheets of plywood and about as thick as a bread loaf. My name was on both of them.

What in the world can that be? I thought. *A sailing dinghy? Bookcases? He's never given me anything this big before. What's going on?*

His wife came in. "Hi, Senior!"

I hugged her and wished her a Merry Christmas. "Where's the boy?"

"Outside. He's playing with the neighbor's kids. Can I get you something?"

"Coffee."

"Alright, but don't open your present until I get back. No peeking!"

"I promise."

She left.

"What's in it, son? You get rich or something?"

"Oh, no! It seems big, but it didn't cost much. I made it myself."

'Vina brought my coffee. I set it down and went over by the tree. "Can I open them now?"

The front door slammed as forty-five pounds of energy came banging through.

"Hi, Grandpa!"

Both parents grabbed for him and shushed him. His mother said, "Grandpa's going to open his present now. You just wait a minute."

All three of them stood there, grinning at me.

"Go ahead, now," said Junior.

As soon as I moved it away from the wall, I knew what it was. My rocks. He'd built cases for my rocks. I tore the paper off. He'd done a beautiful job. Each shelf was wired for lights and carpeted in dark velveteen. Behind clear plastic doors, the collection looked proud indeed, and worthy of its new purpose.

"I don't know what to say," I stammered. "Thanks. I had no idea."

"We were afraid that you were going to miss the rocks, and start asking questions," grinned Junior.

"Who, me? I mean, why should I miss them? I mean, I guess I did miss them, but I figured you had them all along, so I wasn't worried. As a matter of fact, you may well open your present now. It's the rest of the rocks."

"Well, I'll be darned! I was right then. There were some rocks missing. That's okay. There's plenty of room in the cabinets for expanding your collection."

"Your collection, son. That's your Christmas present from me. Sorry I don't have a card to go with it. I even intended to write you a letter, but I didn't get around to it."

"Are you serious?"

"Sure, I'm serious. These rocks, they kind of make a bridge for you and me. Close off all the empty space between us. Maybe you and your sons will need a bridge someday. Anyway, they're yours. I'll even help you make cards for them."

"Thanks, Dad."

"Think nothing of it."

"I love you."

"I love you, too."

Cutting Loose

Henrietta, at her age, looked better than women who were ten to twenty years younger. The envy of her peer group, she was in love. It didn't matter that the man she loved received a small total disability check as his sole source of income, or that he fancied himself a poet, or that he was manic-depressive; he was a man and she loved him.

However, years of inactivity and prolonged depression, in spite of his medication, had caused Walter to lose his self-esteem.

Instead of loving himself, he depended on Henrietta's love as a reason for his existence. And, instead of being grateful for her love, he resented it. He refused to marry her.

****

Henrietta stepped of the bathroom scales residing in the spare bedroom she used as a dressing room. Nude, she ran in place vigorously. She raised her knees as high as they could go, her breasts flopping like pears on a broomstick handle. Her dark hair bobbed like a bird's nest in a high wind. She sang as she entered the shower:

"Tra la la la, no gain for me!

I'm just as happy as I can be!"

She dressed in cotton panties, pantyhose (which Walter called chastity belts, and thought they should have snap crotches), a padded bra, and a slip. She chose a green, calf-length dress with a belt. She sat in front of a three-mirrored dresser to wistfully examine the wrinkles that accented her changing beauty.

She greeted the day with a smile as she stepped out into the morning sunshine. She still smiled as she began the swift walk to work, which was a mile and a half away. Halfway there, she stopped in at a dilapidated house on the edge of the industrial district. Four noses, pressed against the dirty window panes that overlooked the grass yard, disappeared in a flurry of noise.

"Miss Henry's here!" they squealed, and stumbled into each other on their way out the door to greet her. She gave each of them a stick of gum and a dime.

"Enjoy the chewing gum and save your money until you have enough to buy something you really want," she advised, and then entered the house.

Only shafts of sunlight reached inside. Wherever they touched, there was disorder and damage. The walls were streaked with crayons and pocked white from assorted missiles. The stuffed chair and sofa were worn through at the arms and stained with unrecognizable stains. Toys, papers, and coloring books were scattered everywhere. In the kitchen, slim, fourteen-year-old Morina stood with fists on hips. She smiled a welcome to her visitor and waited to be spoken to.

"Good morning, Morina! I'll take a dozen of your very best cookies. How's little Julito?"

Morina's voice held but a charming trace of a Mexican accent.

"Oh, he's just fine, Miss Henry. He will be three months old next week. He will be strong and healthy like his father."

"Oh, then you really do know who the father is," blurted out Henrietta, and immediately blushed. "Oh, I'm sorry. I didn't mean that the way it sounded. I meant to say, do you know WHERE the father is?"

Morina's smile broadened, white teeth gleaming against dark, smooth skin. "Sure. I know. No need to worry."

"I don't worry my dear. I'm merely interested in your well-being. Is your cookie business going well?"

"Sometimes. Sometimes not so good. It's hard, you know. My parents, they both work, so I have to watch the younger ones and take care of my Julito too. There is not so much time."

"That's a shame, my dear. I'm sure that no one in the world bakes like you do. Someday, you must show me how you do it."

Morina grinned and shook her head. "There is nothing to show. I just do it like my grandmother taught me. It's all in the ingredients. Here's a new batch. These are richer than any I have baked before."

"That's just what I wanted, Morina. Here's your two dollars."

"These cost three dollars, Miss Henry. I use better ingredients now."

Henrietta hesitated before reaching into her purse. She sat the brown paper bag onto the table with other like bags. "Well, all right, but these had better be really good."

"You will like them," grinned Morina. "I know you will."

She turned to put away the money in the bread box, where quite a few other dollars already lay.

****

At break time, Morina's predictions were confirmed.

"Henny, this is the best stuff you've ever baked!" gushed the redhead from the steno pool. "Where on earth did you get the recipe?"

The others signaled their agreement in a chatter of noise that not one of then listened to. Henrietta accepted the praise gracefully, but hungrily. She finished her day flushed by peer approval. Three times that afternoon, she stopped working, leaned against the backrest, closed her eyes, and, while basking in the still-warm memories, ate the remaining three cookies.

"Oh, I'm just as happy as can be," she sang. "Tra la la la, tra la la lee." She danced around her desk as she shut down for the day.

Her supervisor, accompanied by a cascade of the latest experiment in Madison Avenue Musk, peered at Henrietta through the bifocal part of the rhinestone glasses that normally hung from her neck by an eighteen-karat, solid gold safety chain (that everyone knew about because she told everyone about it). Henrietta unwrinkled her nose as she turned to face the intruder.

"Yes, Mrs. VanOften?"

"I've heard a lot about the wonderful treats you've been baking for our staff. We're having a regional meeting at my home the day after tomorrow. Do you think that you would be kind enough to bake something for us? Six dozen would be fine. We'll pay for the materials, of course, and give you something for your time."

Henrietta's head swam, as she agreed to do it for five dollars per dozen over cost. The supervisor hesitated, and then agreed, saying, "Alright, but they'd better be really good."

"They will be. You'll like them, I'm sure."

****

On her way home, she stopped again at the paintless house with the falling porch.

"I need six dozen of your very best, Morina, by tomorrow night or early the next morning. Will you do that for me?"

"No, I don't think so, Miss Henry. Already, I have too many orders."

"I'll pay you, let's see, three dollars and fifty cent a dozen," promised Henrietta.

"Three fifty? No. For four dollars, I make you three dozen. You can have them tomorrow morning."

Henrietta smiled her agreement and began happily recalculating her profit as she left to return to her apartment. Walter was there. He wanted money. She reluctantly gave him ten dollars, knowing that he would leave immediately to spend it. It dampened her spirits only a little bit.

****

The next morning, she followed exactly the same routine as she had the morning before. She gave the kids their treats and dimes and bought a dozen cookies for break time.

"I'll pick up the special order on my way home from work, Morina."

"That be fine, Miss Henry."

Morina sat down the bag that Henrietta handed her while she rummaged through her purse for her money. Neither of them noticed that she picked up the wrong bag on her way out the door.

At break time, when she dumped them from the brown paper bag onto the tray beside the coffee urn, she failed to notice, since she was chatting with a friend at the same time, that the cookies were pornographic. Vulvas, penises, and copulating couples displayed their sugared splendor without shame.

Henrietta was mortified at first – until the girls began laughing and grabbing for their favorite cookies. They praised her daring and questioned the source of her anatomical knowledge. She shrugged off their curiosity with a blushing, "I'll never tell," and accepted their praise with a brand new intensity of enjoyment. For the first time ever, there was not a cookie left for her to enjoy in the afternoon.

It was about two o'clock when Mrs. VanOften stopped by again. She was smiling.

"I understand that you brought some unusual cookies today, Henrietta."

"Uh, yes. I did. I'm afraid that there aren't any left, though."

"Oh no, my dear. That's quite alright. I just wanted to ask if you would bake mine in the same fashion – discreetly, of course.

Regional is always looking for someone who stands out from the ranks, if you know what I mean?"

Henrietta remembered Morina's earlier reluctance. She looked at her supervisor's fixed stare and smiled and fumbled for a way to say no.

"I don't see how – there just isn't time. Maybe more money?"

"Money is no object, dear. I'll be glad to pay fifty dollars over your cost for fifteen dozen."

"Fifty dollars! I'll try, Mrs. VanOften. That's all I can do."

"Nonsense. Only losers 'try.' Here's fifty dollars. Let me know what your expenses are. I'll expect the cookies no later than six tomorrow evening. Fifteen dozen, not six. And I want sugar cookies, my dear; the crisp kind. Thank you, dear. I admire your courage and openness. Regional has a place for those qualities."

The supervisor left the office. Henrietta wrinkled her nose, took a can of telephone disinfectant from the desk drawer, and sprayed it around her office to mask the smell of strong perfume.

"Fifty dollars? What can I buy for fifty dollars?"

Morina turned her down flat. Even a twenty five dollar bonus would not sway her.

"Julito's father is coming tonight. Not even for a hundred dollars would I bake cookies tonight. No way. Listen. Why don't you bake them? I could let you use the cutters. You could do it," she encouraged.

"Oh, but I never could."

"Really? How long have you been dead?"

"Well, I mean, I don't know your ingredients, do I?"

"I'll sell you the cookie dough. For twenty-five dollars, you can have the dough."

"But I have no cookie sheets, and I only have one oven. You have three."

Morina's hands went to her hips. "Listen," she said, "Julito's father is coming. I need the money for him. You give me the twenty five dollars, and I give you everything you need. With just one oven, you have to stay up a little later, that's all. OK?"

"Well, I guess so."

"Here. Here are the cutters. I get you the cookie sheets. If you want to get fancy, you can make whatever you want different colors. Just add a little vegetable dye to the dough, you see."

"Where did you get these, if I may ask?"

"My fifth brother. He is a silversmith, but these are not silver – they are tin."

She opened the refrigerator and pulled out five plastic bags of whitish colored dough.

"Here's your cookie dough. These dough, they are what my grandmother used. Where's my money?"

"Here you are, Morina. Is there anything else I need, or need to know?"

"Rub butter, not margarine on the sheet, and don't bake them too long. Will you excuse me now? I want to get ready."

"Oh, dear. Yes. Well, goodbye, Morina. I hope you have a pleasant evening."

"You too, Miss Henny. You too."

Henrietta practically screamed as her boyfriend, Walter, walked in and touched her on the shoulder. She was rapt in her examination of the complete collection of cookie cutters and she let her attention get so focused on one particular shape that she completely missed his entrance.

"Walter," she gasped. "My God! You practically scared me to death."

Walter seemed scared too, the way he scuttled back from her sudden spin. He was not as tall as she, and much skinnier.

"Me too," he said. "Whatcha got there?"

"Oh, nothing," she said.

Instead of convincing him, his curiosity was aroused, and after a brief tussle, he succeeded in making her let go of the cutter. He studied the piece for an instant, turning it over in his hands, trying to figure out what it was. When it dawned on him, a series of expressions flashed across his fact: disbelief, amusement, a quizzical look, an 'aha!' look, and finally a look of canniness and wile that no one had ever told him about, but all had often seen.

"Where did you git these?" he half asked, half demanded.

He spotted and grabbed the brown paper bag, dumping it onto her kitchen table and pawing through the cutters, whistling at this one, chuckling at the one, giving Henrietta a lewd wink over another one.

"You've been holding out on me, Henny," he said in a mock-aggrieved tone.

"No, I...quit it, Walter. Give those back. It's not what you think."

"Oh yeah?" he grinned. "What about this?"

He held a cutter up to shoulder height. "This can't be anything but what it looks like it is. We ought to try this one Henny, like over and over and over."

"Quit it, Walter, or I'm going to get mad."

Her voice was sharp. Walter became instantly conciliatory.

"Sure. Here, honey. I was only kidding. What do you have these for, really?"

She told him the story. He snickered all the way through it and burst out laughing as she ended the story with getting the ingredients from Morina.

"Here you are," he said, "the world's greatest prude, selling x-rated eat-em-ups, lewd food, and all for a pat on the back from some dame that wants to make a social hit. Tell you what, Henny, why don't we just make up a special batch of cookies for ourselves, go to bed with them, and let nature take its course?"

"Quit saying I'm a prude," she said. "I was married before, you know."

"I know, I know. To a warrior with a bent sword and no spine."

He caught the stare of anger that was building up in Henrietta's face. "Oh, jeez, I'm sorry. I shouldn't have said that. But dammit, Henry, I'm a man too. I got feelings too."

"I know, Walter. I'm sorry too, but I just don't love you like that anymore."

Walter's face froze in position. He handed the sack back to her. "Anything I can do to help?" he asked, his voice cold.

She took no notice of the change in him. "You're sweet. Thanks, Walter. I'd love to have your help. You can melt some butter for me. One stick will be fine. Be careful not to burn it though."

Walter busied himself with the task, saying nothing. She also worked silently, intent on doing everything right the first time.

"How much are you getting?" asked Walter.

"What?"

"How much are you getting for all this work?"

"Fifty dollars," she answered absentmindedly.

"Fifty dollars!" he yelled. "Hey kiddo, we got ourselves a gold mine here." He left the butter pan on the burner, and went straight for her, forcing her to abandon what she was doing, and devote her full attention to him. She didn't turn willingly, but he was stronger.

"What do you want?" she snapped, her face scowling.

"A gold mine, Henny. That's what we got here. I'll bet I could sell fifty dozen a week down at the pool hall alone."

"Well, that's fifty dollars for six dozen, Walter, less the ingredients. That's about...almost...let's see..."

"$8.33 a dozen. I can git a dollar apiece, twelve bucks a dozen. That's $3.67 a dozen, times fifty dozen, make that a hundred dozen, that's three hundred and sixty seven dollars every two weeks just from the pool hall. If I could do just ten more hangouts, that's be over fifteen a week. Wow. I could afford to get married!"

Henrietta stopped resisting immediately. "Do you mean that? If we could make...if you could make fifteen hundred a week, we could be married?"

"I didn't say...I mean...I suppose so. It's possible. Anything's possible."

Henrietta took that for affirmation. "Oh, Walter," she said. "You're so sweet. No wonder I love you. The butter's burning."

"Oh, jeez," he said. "Excuse me."

He disengaged from her sudden embrace, and gave his full attention to rescuing the butter.

"I could sell two or three dozen a week at the office," she said. "I'll talk to Morina. Maybe her brother can make us another set of cookie cutters, and she can furnish the mixes. Does that sound alright, honey?"

"All right? Yeah. That sounds alright. Ok. Hey, listen. Can you do the rest of this yourself? I.thought of some things I have to do."

"Sure, honey. I can do it just fine."

He kissed the tip of her nose on his way out the door. "I'll call you."

"All right, honey. Goodbye."

****

Mrs. VanOften's home stood out among the neighbors both by being the only one on a small hill, and by being noticeably larger, having fireplace chimney stacks at both ends. Henrietta parked in the street and walked the half block long path to the front door. The door opened on the third ring.

"Oh, good," gushed Mrs. VanOften. "The cookies are here. Was it much trouble, my dear?"

"No, ma'am. I just had to stay up later is all. I've got the rest of them in the car. Do you want to take these?"

"Oh, why, here, my dear. Just take them into the kitchen while I find some suitable plates."

Henrietta followed her. The double doors to the parlor were open, so Henrietta sneaked a peek. A dozen or so women milled about the party, with goodies offered throughout the room. The only male, a bartender, was handing a drink to a willowy blond dressed, as all of them were, in business sensibles. Henrietta sat the packages on the counter and left to bring in the rest of them. On her way out, one of the guests stopped her.

"Hi! What did you just bring in?"

"Some cookies. I have to go get the rest of them."

When she returned, five women were in the kitchen, examining the shapes with giggles and glee, and calling to the others to come see. Mrs. VanOften's smile of happiness was as real as it had ever been. Only one woman, the shortest and oldest looking of them all, was not smiling. Her face was frozen into a disapproving mask. She was starting at Mrs. VanOften. As Henrietta laid the other packages down, she spoke sharply.

"That's quite enough of this. Are you responsible for this, Grace?"

Mrs. VanOften's smile tumbled like a broken kite.

"I...why....I..."

"Get them out of here at once! You, girl! You take these back to your bakery and think about being boycotted by every decent person I know."

"I don't have a bakery, Mrs. Roman. I work under Mrs. VanOften."

"You do, eh? Well, you don't any longer. You may stop by Monday to clear out your desk. Your severance check will be mailed to you."

"It isn't my fault, Mrs. Roman. Mrs. VanOften ordered them and paid me fifty dollars for them."

"I never ordered any such thing, Henrietta. When I spoke of your unusual cookies, I was referring to the quality, not the loathsome shapes you have brought. I'm sorry, my dear. There's nothing I can do. Take your cookies and go."

Henrietta, in a state of shock, dumped the platters into the sack and carried them in one load back to the car. As she passed the double doors, every eye in the room watched. Not one face smiled.

****

Henrietta cried for most of the night. Walter woke her at seven AM by pounding on her door. She donned her floor-length, purple robe, fixed her hair with her hands, and let him in.

"Oh, Walter," she said as soon as she saw him. "I've been fired."

Walter returned her hug, patting her on the back while she rested her chin on his shoulder.

"Why don't you fix us some coffee?" he asked. "Then we can sit down and talk about it."

She served him coffee at the kitchen table, and placed a bag of cookies in the middle. "You may as well eat these. They're what got me fired."

Walter reached into the bag, drew out a penis, and ate it without noticing, so closely he listened to her tale.

"What do you plan to do with the cookies?" he asked.

"Take them back to Morina, I guess. Maybe she can sell them for me."

"Don't be stupid," he snapped.

Henrietta's lips tightened.

"Morina won't take them back. She'd be selling your stuff in competition with her own."

Her shoulders slumped another half inch. "I never thought of that. What am I going to do, Walter?"

"Say that again."

"What?"

"What you just said."

"I said I never thought of that."

"No, I mean after that."

"I don't know what I said."

"Yes, you do. You said, 'What am I going to do, Walter,' that's what you said."

"So what?"

"So, if you really want me to tell you what to do, I will."

"Oh, Walter, I'm so scared. I'm over forty. Wherever could I find another good job?"

Walter got up, walked to the back of her chair, and began massaging her shoulders. "Leave it to me, Henny. Now here's what I want you to do."

His hands slid down beneath the front of her robe. She held his wrists.

"I want you to go to bed with me right now. Your troubles are over. Walter will take care of everything. You just have to take care of Walter."

Her shoulders collapsed. "All right, Walter," she sighed. "You can have me if you want."

She lay quite still on the bed while he did.

"Ahhh! That was great!" he said as he put on his pants.

"Now, I'm gonna sell some cookies. How many are there?" he asked on the way to the kitchen.

"Fifteen dozen."

Walter began putting the bags into a large grocery bag. He sat the fifth bag aside until he was done. He opened it and counted the cookies. "There's only seven in this bag. Did you eat any?"

"No," came dully from the bedroom.

"Well, I ate one, so that means your fancy ladies ripped off four of them...unless Morina shorted you."

She came into the kitchen. "Probably five. The one you ate came from a different bag, do you'll be short in one more bag. Morina is very good."

"Fifteen times twelve is 185 dollars. Less five, no six, leaves 171 dollars. Half is eight-five fifty. Would eight-five fifty make you feel any better?"

She pulled her open, dragging robe together as a look of alertness came back to her face. "Yes, Walter, it would. A lot."

"Bye, babe."

He gave her a henpeck on the lips, and left, whistling.

****

The screaming, crying, and occasional thuds carried easily from the open door to the broken, weedy sidewalk in front of Morina's house. The ten AM sun was already sweltering. Henrietta's blouse stuck to her skin as she got out of the car. She went forward slowly, stopping frequently to listen, but understanding no words of the Spanish phrases that came tumbling around her ears. She listened again at the screen door until there was a lull. She knocked. No answer. She knocked again.

"Morina?"

Some rustling noises came from the kitchen.

"Morina, are you alright?"

"Yes, Miss Henny. I'm all right."

Behind her stood a youth, smooth-cheeked and well built, but with a weak moustache. He glared at the back of Morina's head, and then at Henrietta.

"What is it you want, Miss Henny?" asked Morina.

"I brought back your cookie sheets. I baked the cookies, but the head lady didn't like them, so she fired me, and Walter is selling them for eighty-five dollars and fifty cents, so now I'm going into business with him, and make lots of money, and getting married and everything! Isn't that wonderful? I just wanted to get your recipe for the cookie dough, and find out if you can get some cookie cutters made for me and maybe bake some while I'm getting things together."

Morina put her hands on her hips and stepped backwards a half step around so that she could see the youth and Henrietta just by turning her head. She looked at the youth.

"See, Julio? So what if you lost your job. You don't look like eighteen. You look like sixteen, like you are. You won't get no job in

Texas – just more peons, like you are. Stay here with me and Julito. I will bake, and you can sell, just like Miss Henny."

Julio spoke in a voice trembling with anger. "Sure. And maybe I bring you in washing to do, and mending of other people's clothes. Or maybe I go pimp for you, and bring you ugly old men."

Morina slapped him. "Go, then, you baby pig! Go and try to find diamonds in shit. But don't you ever come back to me!"

Julio smiled, saluted grotesquely, and brushed hard against Henrietta as he left. Henrietta recovered her balance, moved to where Morina stood frozen, and hugged her until the crying stopped.

"Please sit down, Miss Henny. Maybe we should talk."

****

"Walter, I can't afford you," said Henrietta.

"What the hell are you talking about?"

"Fifty percent is too much. By the time I pay for the ingredients and the electricity and everything, I'd be making about fifty dollars a week."

"Who the hell have you been talking to?"

"Morina."

"Yeah, well, you listen to me. You said you wanted my help, and by God, you're going to get it. Maybe it will only be fifty dollars at first, but I'll built it up to a hundred and fifty in no time."

"Yes, but you'll be making all the money."

"Expenses, baby, expenses." He approached her. "Don't worry about it. Come to bed. I'll make you feel better."

"No thank you, Walter. I feel quite all right. I've decided that I can only pay you twenty percent commission."

"YOU can only pay ME!" he exploded. "Try this: Walter is the only one who can make something out of this cookie business. Or Walter can leave me alone and watch me sink like a piece of dirty toilet paper."

"Can you get me three more ovens, Walter?"

He stared without reply.

"I thought not. Every bill collector in town is after you, and you haven't held a job in the three years I've known you. Just where do you get your money for living, Walter?"

"I hustle, baby. Just like I can hustle your cookies."

"You can...if you'll accept twenty percent."

"Unh unh, baby. Fifty percent, or nothing."

"Then I'm afraid it's nothing, Walter."

"Yeah, well, that's OK by me. There's lots of younger women around, and well, frankly, you're a bum lay, Henny. You ought to read a book. See you around."

As he left, Henrietta stood there, unmoving. She listened to his steps going down the hall. When the front door closed, she began taking off her nightclothes as she danced around the room. By the time she got under the shower, she was singing:

> Tra la la la la, tra la la lee,
>
> I'm just as happy as I can be.
>
> Thank you, Lord, for sending Morina to me,
>
> Tra la la la la la lee!

Cutting Loose

The Predators

Her eyes, lustrous brown, alert, expressive, and brightened by unfallen tears, closed against the pain.

Deep in the ravine, there was no wind. A squirrel frisked over the newly fallen snow, heading in my direction. I thumbed off the safety on my four-ten shotgun.

"Hi counselor! Oh, oh. What's wrong?"

"Nothing. Nothing is wrong. How are you doing?"

"Just fine. I'm still off grass."

"Good."

She dabbed at her eyes with a tissue, and then blew her nose into it.

The snow fell in quiet beauty, with only the occasional shoosh as some fell from an overburdened branch. The squirrel was still on the opposite side of the ravine, still out of range.

"Why don't you tell me what's the matter?"

"We're here to discuss your problems, not mine."

"That isn't fair. We're been together for four months now. I never dreamed we could be so close in such a short time."

"That's because of you. You're a very special man."

The squirrel stopped, sat erect, and smelled the air around him. I didn't move a muscle.

"This is our last session together."

An emotion whipped through my body. I couldn't decipher it at first, but soon decided it was fear. I didn't know what to say.

"They're not renewing my contract. Budget cuts. Three weeks before Christmas. I had to take all the gifts I bought back to the stores."

"Budget-cutting bureaucrats. More money for the general's pot."

"I don't even know the man who signed my dismissal. I feel like he's some huge animal that pounced on me out of the bushes."

The squirrel disappeared behind a tree. Perhaps he had a hole there where he would be safe.

She smiled. "Well, how are you doing? All ready for the holidays?"

"I dread them. We're visiting in-laws, people I don't really know. I see a week of misery ahead."

In a vee where a branch met a trunk, a nose and two bright eyes appeared, staring straight at me without seeing me. I waited, still as a snowman.

"What's the problem?"

"Three of them still smoke grass. I may be tempted beyond endurance."

"You will always be tempted. Perhaps this is the trial that proves your resolve."

"That's a good way to view it. Thanks."

The squirrel ran up the far side of the trunk, and then back to the ground on the near side. I slowly shifted the gun.

"Four months without marijuana. Aren't you proud?"

"No. I miss it too much."

"Well, I'm proud of you."

"This will be the first Christmas in thirty-five years that I haven't been drunk, high, or both."

"Wow."

"Yeah. Wow."

He ran the rest of the way down the far side of the ravine, and vanished behind some clumps of snow-decorated shrubbery. Very carefully, I moved the butt of the shotgun up to my shoulder, muzzle still pointed to the ground.

"Your fiancée is a lucky woman to have you."

"I wish I believed that. We're totally opposite of each other."

"That's a blessing."

"How so?"

"If you don't try to change each other, you can be each other's source of strength and hope."

"Like a booster club?"

"Something like that."

"Thanks. I see what you mean."

The squirrel appeared again, still heading in my direction.

"You have to think about replacing me."

"After you, there can be no others."

"Thanks for the charm, but you really ought to consider it."

"I have considered it. I want to try it on my own. I'm tired of depending on others. I want to be free of counselors and therapists."

"That's a great goal. Our meeting is over. I'm not saying goodbye. I'm afraid I'm going to lose it."

"Me too. Hug?"

We hugged, clinging to each other, trying to be brave enough not to let go.

"In one of my stories, we meet and depart with a kiss on the forehead."

She pulled my head down and kissed my brow. I kissed hers.

"Goodbye."

"Goodbye."

The squirrel ran up a small bush, stopped, and looked straight at me. I moved the shotgun muzzle up. He stayed motionless. I squeezed the trigger. He dropped to the snow, instantly dead. It was a big, fat, gray squirrel, perfect for the pot.

Jonathon

For a while, I was both boss and friend to the biggest Northern Pike that ever swam the waters of the St. Croix river, which is a boundary water between Minnesota and Wisconsin. If only we had stayed friends, I might have been rich.

He was a beautiful fish. His green body was speckled with gold flecks and his head had the brilliance of fire opal. But his eyes were mean. Jonathon had no mercy anywhere in his twelve foot body.

I wasn't even fishing when I caught him. All I did was throw out my anchor after I beached my houseboat at my favorite spot on the river. He must have thought my anchor was a bird. He didn't even give it a chance to hit the water. Like huge clam shells, his terrible jaws clamped down on it, and he was hooked.

For fourteen hours I fought to keep him from dragging my boat from shore where it was tied to two small willows. Blisters as big as golf balls grew on my palms; when they broke, they left angry, red flesh behind. Still, I fought on.

The spray of the water kicked up by his tail kept the anchor chain cool and created a lot of rainbows. It was like being inside of one. By the time dusk came, he was still going strong. The anchor chain was turning red close to his mouth. I feared it would soon melt. I was ready to abandon ship, when a horde of Minnesota mosquitoes flew by, so thick and huge that they looked like a flock of geese in the fall. All of that fighting had made Jonathon hungry. He jumped and started gulping them. It made them so mad that they stung him until he was half dead. They didn't bother me, because the spray from his jumping fell around me the whole time. As soon as he quit feeding, they quit too, and flew north to feed on moose.

Before Jonathon could recover, I took some two-inch hawser line I had salvaged from a derelict towboat, and ran it into the back of one set of gills and out the back of the other. That gave me reins, like on a horse, plus something to tie him to the back of my boat, which I did, and hurriedly retied the boat to stronger trees. He couldn't swim away, and he couldn't close his gills. Now he was mine.

Jonathon floated belly-up for a long time after I tied him up. I watched him until the full moon was in the middle of the sky. I was too tired to see if he'd survive, so I went to bed.

The next morning, the cove was so white, it looked like there was snow floating on it. Hundreds of bodies of silver bass filled every inch. All of their heads were gone, and their bellies were missing. Jonathon had done it. My Great Northern Pike had proved that he was as tough as he was mean.

As near as I could figure, word had gotten out that Jonathon was caught and tied. Huge schools of silver came by to rejoice at the site of their enemy. They had no way of knowing that his tether was a hundred feet long.

That incident taught me that Jonathon killed for sport as well as food. One nibble from his mighty jaws, lined with hundreds of needle-sharp teeth, neatly severed the heads from the bass. The next nibble completely removed their bellies. That's all he ate – heads and bellies. The rest of the fish were mine just for dipping them out of the water.

I never had such easy fish to fry. Two swift passes of the knife, and I had filets so fresh that they practically flopped in the frying pan that morning. But I had never learned to keep my mouth shut. I told every fisherman that came my way about how Jonathon had learned to float belly up until the silver bass came to gloat, and how he cleaned them out. Soon, the lumberjacks started coming by for fish dinners, and to see the great pike.

I thought I had it made. I didn't have to spend a dime for gas or bait. Jonathon, like a big, friendly dog, learned to pull my houseboat through the water to all the best fishing spots. The lumberjacks emptied their wallets as they filled their bellies. But the jacks began wanting walleye. Trouble was, there wasn't enough walleye to feed them and Jonathon too.

I got around it at first by only taking my pike out after he'd filled up on silvers. Then his heart wasn't in killing, so he'd send me up a few dozen ten and twelve pounders out of reflex meanness, I guess. It was OK though, until the silver bass came close to becoming an endangered species, and Jonathon developed a taste for walleye. I knew the end was near when he left me one measly fifteen pounder to feed a forest full of growling stomachs.

I was on my knees, pleading with them not to eat Jonathon, when a school of upper-river silvers chased a school of minnows into the bay, and the slaughter began. It saved his life that day. The lumberjacks went back to their trees with their bellies full of bass. But they left me with an ultimatum. Feed us walleye, or we eat Jonathon.

I tried to make Jonathon understand. "Fish," I said, "you and me's got to reach an understanding. You've got a better life than you've ever dreamed of, and you've got me to take care of you."

Jonathon stared at me through the open railing gate. He suddenly seemed so sensitive and intelligent. I sensed that he wanted his freedom. "Tell you what I'll do. You lay off eating all those walleye, and when the season's done, and the ice comes, I'll set you free."

He flicked his tail gently enough to barely raise a swell. His eyes seemed to soften even more, and I wondered if he really understood.

The next morning, we went after walleye. He started sending up fifteen and twenty pounders by the bushel basket full. I flourished. Merchants came from far and wide to buy my surplus.

I was true to my word. Late that fall, all the merchants and lumberjacks gathered to watch me set Jonathon free. I put on my finest duds, and strapped on my pistol case in case someone wanted to steal him. I'd also fire off a goodbye salute when he left for the big waters.

Jonathon knew something big was about to happen. He kept his back and head out of the water, and watched the men on shore like he wished he had legs. His eyes were again meaner and crueler than ever.

We were celebrating so much that by the time I got ready to let him go, the jacks had fed me so much distilled pine juice that I could hardly stand up.

"Jonathon, old buddy," I slobbered, "you and me's been great pals. Now it's time to say goodbye. Goodbye, Jonathon, old friend."

As I slipped the last yard of hawser line from his gills, I leaned over to kiss him goodbye.

He bit off my nose.

I shot him. We had Jonathon steaks all winter. Too bad. He might have made me rich. He'd have come back next spring. I just know he would have.

Jack Dukes

The following stories are about episodes in my life that are too sensitive to face head-on: marriage, infidelity, divorce, growth, escape, recovery, and more. The analogies are from my book, *Without Apology.*

The Golden Pheasants

A dozen shotgun pellets tore into the left side of the flying Golden Pheasant. As he tumbled to earth in a powder puff of feathers, a female Golden Pheasant was hit in her right side. Both of them, though badly wounded and disfigured, found refuge from the dogs and hunters in abandoned groundhog tunnels.

They lay still for days, letting Nature heal them. While they rested, they thought of the pheasant farm where they had been raised. Both of them came from the same place, though neither one knew the other was alive. Both of them had the same dreams and memories.

When they were hatched, they didn't know they were special, but the goddess who took care of them knew. She kept them in special cages where people who visited the farm could see their rare beauty. There were some good times, like the egg-fertilization times, but they never fertilized eggs together, and the female Golden Pheasant was never allowed to hatch her own eggs.

Their special cages allowed them to see over the entire farm. They didn't have much to do, so they watched and learned the routines. Some of the birds, they saw, were put into crates, loaded into a truck, and driven away, often long past the middle of the night. They were always the finest birds on the farm, and the Golden Pheasants longed to go with them.

They watched some of the birds being carried into a special building. They never came out again. They didn't know for sure what went on in there, but the songs that leaked through to their special cages were sad songs. They both knew they didn't want to go there, but then they learned that there was no place else to go. All the birds that hatched when they did were going there now, cage by cage.

The Golden Pheasants were sad at first, and began humming the same sad song that came from the special building without realizing it, but, because they were Golden Pheasants, they kept scheming about how to get into the crates. They wished as hard as they could for it. No one can say for sure whether their wishing had anything to do with it, but one day, the goddess forgot to latch their cages. When the pickup came with its crates that night, their cage doors opened with a single peck. They sailed down to be caught and loaded into separate crates aboard the truck.

The wind of the speeding truck made every feather alive with anticipation. Then it slowed, and the ride became very bumpy. One by one, the crates were emptied. The Golden Pheasants ran into a field ripe with seeds better than goddess had ever given them and full of places to hide and sit, places to run and be free. They sang songs to urge the sun up so that they could learn more about their new world. The sun was up for only a few minutes when the shotgun blasts tumbled them out of the sky.

****

The Golden Pheasants saw each other for the first time on a gravel road that bordered their field. He saw her good left side out of his good right eye, and she saw his good right side out of her good left eye. They fell in love at once, and wanted to nest together right away, but something made them hesitate.

"I am no longer perfect," they each though. "If I show my ugly side, the other will run away."

They worked nearer and nearer to each other each day, but always with their good sides showing. Neither of them wanted to lose the other, even though they only chatted.

One day, the farmer came along and plowed up their homes. That's when he saw her ugly side. She flew into such a rage that she forgot to hide herself, and didn't notice him watching. When she was done, he sidled up to her, still showing his best side, and introduced himself for the first time.

"Hello, I'm Herman. I was hatched on a pheasant farm where goddess lives. I almost wish I was back there now."

"Me too! I'm Shiela." She was still angry and didn't want to talk much. She also was afraid that he had seen her ugly side. "Were you watching? If you were, I'll hate you for it."

"Yes, I watched. I saw your ugly side."

She croaked a bitter song and ran off into the woodlands at the side of the plowed field, before he could show her his ugly side. He ran after her, but his leg was hurt worse than her, and he could not catch up.

"Wait, Shiela! Don't run away! I have an ugly side too!"

But she did not believe him, and ran over a hill and out of his view. He tried to find her, but could not. All night long, he probed the woods and called to her. When daybreak came, he was tired and rested on his bad side so only his good side would show, as was his custom. That's how Shiela saw him when she got up to go get some gravel.

"Oh, Herman," she whispered. "You are the most beautiful rooster I have ever seen. Why did you tell me you were ugly?" And she walked away towards the road without disturbing him.

Herman wanted some gravel too, when he awoke a little later. By now, he had resigned himself to losing Shiela. When he reached the road, the first thing he saw out of his bad left eye was an ugly, disfigured bird. Out of her bad right eye, she too saw an ugly, disfigured bird.

"Hello, I'm Shiela. I see that you're ugly like I am. Would you like to fertilize my eggs?"

Herman turned his neck to see her better, and recognized her right away. "Hello, Shiela. Will you nest with me if I do?"

Shiela recognized his voice and screamed, "Herman! You really are ugly! I thought you were lying to me. Of course I'll nest with you now. Do you think our chicks will be ugly too?"

"No, Shiela. I think that they will be splendid…just like we used to be."

They walked down the road to a new field, their ugly sides touching so that all that the world could see was their beauty.

****

Their new field was better than the one before. It was alive with bugs to chase, with rabbits, and with birds that sang to them all day long.

"Oh, Herman! When I think of all we missed by being on the pheasant farm, I forget all about my bad side."

"Me too, Shiela. It was beautiful to have goddess bring us food and care for our chicks, but it is much nicer to find our own."

"Herman, I have something to show you. Come with me to our nest."

Herman followed willingly, enjoying listening to her chatter.

"While you were gone today, Herman, I did something special. I hope you'll be proud of me. See, Herman? Two of them!"

Herman looked at the two eggs in the nest and began laughing as loud as he could.

"Chicks! We're going to have our own chicks, and the goddess can't take them away from us! Oh Shiela, you are the most special bird of all the birds that are."

He moved so that the feathers of his good side touched the feathers on her good side, and made them both feel warm and comfortable. The next morning, Shiela didn't want to go with him into the fields. Herman didn't mind. "I have to go, though. I have to find someone to tell the good news to."

"I understand, Herman. You go on now."

Herman bounced away, squawking back at the other bird's songs. They didn't understand him, of course, but Herman didn't care. He was looking for a pheasant to talk to. He was almost on the other side of the field before he found one. It was an ordinary rooster with a fine ring around his neck, but at least the rooster could understand him.

"Hi, I'm Herman. My mate laid two eggs in one day, and we're going to have chicks," he bragged.

"Big deal. You'd better shut your beak or you'll never see your chicks hatch. There's a fox over there."

"What's a fox?"

"If you're really that dumb, just watch and you'll find out."

Herman watched. The gray fox was crouched almost to the ground. It moved forward a few inches and then, all in the same instant, pulled its lips back from its teeth like white icicles, and jumped square upon a hen pheasant sitting so quietly in the grass that Herman didn't even see her until the last second. He watched the fox bite the hen in the head, and, while she flopped around dying, saw it crack open the eggs she had been sitting on and lick their insides clean.

"Quickly now, Herman. We're safe for a little while. Come with me."

Herman followed without answering, without even thinking. The ring-necked pheasant ran from one clump of grass to another, never going out into the open, never moving more than a few feet at a time, and listening and watching each time that he stopped. Finally, he ran into a clump of grass and disappeared. Herman ran into it too, and found a groundhog tunnel.

"We're safe here, Herman. I'm Roger. Now do you know what a fox is?"

"I sure do. I'm glad we live on the other side of the field."

"You're really dumb. You're a handsome bird, alright, but really dumb. Are you one of those farm pheasants?"

"Yes. Goddess never let a fox get into the farm. Whose eggs were those?"

"Mine, but it's OK. I've got more. I've got twelve hens in my harem...well, it's eleven now; it was twelve. That's all right. I'll find another one. How many are in your flock?"

"One. Shiela."

"One! Dumb! Really dumb! You'll never get any chicks to live that way. Tell you what, Herman. The fox ate the last two rooster friends I had in this field. You visit me every day or two, and I'll teach you how to get along out here. You can even have a couple of my hens."

"No, thank you. I'm happy with Shiela. But I'll come visit you every day, if I can."

Herman kept his word. In return, he learned all that the rooster could tell him. When he told Shiela what the fox did, she became a different bird. She stayed at the nest all the time, except to eat. Herman even had to bring her gravel, because the nearest road was too far away. His leg began hurting so bad that he could not walk without limping. He began complaining. "Sometimes, I wish I'd never fertilized your eggs. Once, I was a partner and friend to you. Now, I am just a slave."

"You go ahead and play, or whatever else you want to do. I must guard my eggs from the fox."

Herman persisted, and she finally agreed to go with him, but only close by. It wasn't all that dangerous, because Hermar knew when the foxes would be full and sleepy, and only took her out at those times. They played a game to see who could find the most interesting thing for the day. Day after day, they lived as if trouble would never visit them again.

Jack Dukes

****

Shiela was the first to spot the trail of golden corn that led up the gravel road and disappeared into a pile of brush along the roadside. She couldn't resist pecking a few kernels before rushing back to tell Herman. "Herman! Come see what I've found!"

Herman was grumpy that morning, and didn't really want to go, but her excitement soon captured him, and he followed her willingly.

"See, Herman? Isn't it lovely?"

Herman had to admit that it was so, and they pecked together all the way up to the brush. Neither one noticed that some of the brushes had no leaves, and were perfectly straight, not at all like the rest of the wood. They were still pecking corn when the trap closed behind them with a clatter that made them squawk in terror.

No one came for them right away. As their fright faded, they realized that they were back in a cage. At first, Herman was quiet. Then he grew angry, and then he flew into a rage like Shiela had when the farmer plowed up their groundhog tunnels.

"See what you got us into?" he shouted, and began beating her about the head with his one good wing. Shiela didn't fight back. She felt badly about what she had done. Instead, she cowered in a corner of the cage, and tucked her head low. Her feelings hurt worse than his blows did, and she waited until his rage was spent.

"I'm sorry, Herman. I didn't know any better."

Herman felt ashamed then, but he didn't know what to say. Instead, he picked out the plumpest kernel of corn and gave it to her out of his own beak. Then, he set about trying to find a way out. He pecked at every bar of the cage. He pecked the floor. He even stood on Shiela's back and tried to push the top away, but nothing worked. Shiela tried too, until both of them became exhausted from their efforts.

When the humans came in their pickup truck, both Golden Pheasants saw right away that it came from the farm where the goddess lived. Soon, they were back on the farm, only this time, they were both put into the same cage. It was a special cage again and as many as had come to see their beauty now came to see their unique ugliness.

****

They had everything that they needed, including each other, but they missed the freedom of their field. Shiela was sadder than Herman. She missed the two eggs she had lain, and worried about what would become of them. Even though she fertilized new eggs, it didn't help, because the goddess took them away as soon as they were laid.

Herman tried to cheer her up, and point out all of the beauty that he could see around them, but she only became sadder. Eventually, she quit talking to him except to complain. She complained about everything. The weather was too hot or too cold, the food was always the same, her wound hurt, his ugliness was too ugly, he didn't show his good side enough.

Herman grew tired of it, and quit fertilizing her eggs. Then, he began complaining back, and they started quarreling. One day, he began beating her again with his good wing. Instead of cowering, she set up such a ruckus that the goddess came and put them into separate cages. The cages were side by side, but they had solid sides so that they could not see each other. They could talk to each other, but four days passed before they began speaking.

"Shiela, do you want to try to escape again? We are no longer happy here."

She did not answer. He tried again.

"Shiela, the first time we escaped, we both wished as hard as we could. Maybe it would work again."

"Do what you want, Herman. I don't care anymore."

Herman tried. He wished as hard as he could, but, without her, his heart wasn't in it, and his cage door stayed locked.

"Shiela, are you wishing?"

"Yes. I'm wishing for my eggs to hatch, and for the chicks to grow up, free from being hunted."

Herman was sad when he heard that, for he knew that it could never be. He tried to tell her so, but she refused to understand.

"First you beat me with your wing, and then you beat me with your words. You have no beauty at all. You are truly the ugliest bird in the world. If you were really beautiful, you would wish my wish."

"I cannot wish for what cannot be, Shiela. I can only wish to be free. Won't you wish that wish with me?"

"No. You are a selfish bird, and I hate you."

Herman shut up then, but he didn't stop wishing. He kept hearing the sad songs from the strange building, and feared that they would be going there soon. He began wishing for both of them, but he did not tell her so. He even asked the other birds that goddess brought to be fertilized to wish with him. They laughed at him. When they left his cage, they talked to the other birds and pointed him out. He didn't know what they said, but they began laughing too. After that, he refused to fertilize them. That's when the goddess came to take him away to the strange building. He began singing the sad song. Shiela heard it.

"Herman, what's happening?"

"I have to go now, Shiela. Goodbye."

"Don't go, Herman. I don't really want to be left alone. Please come back. I will wish your wish."

But it was too late. The goddess was carrying him upside down, holding him by his good and bad legs in just one hand.

"Wish hard, Shiela. Wish harder than you've ever wished before."

Shiela did. Herman did, too. Maybe it was the wishing, or maybe just because his bad leg slipped from the goddess' grasp, but suddenly he fell to the ground. He ran as fast as he could, the goddess right behind him. He ran into a flock of the best birds on the farm, and that slowed the goddess down.

He kept running until he found a small hole in the fence around the farm. No other bird had known it was there, but Herman's freedom in the field had taught him to look for every possible chance to escape from the foxes and hunters. He slipped through, into a field that was almost as pretty as the one he and Shiela had had together.

"Thank you, Shiela, for wishing my wish," he thought, and laid down to rest. Right away, he began thinking of how to get Shiela free, too. He thought all day and all night, and all the next day. Still, he could not find a way to free her. That evening, it started to snow. The wind blew bitter cold, and made his bad side ache for the comfort of a snow nest. He knew he had to leave this field for good, or go back into the farm and risk being captured. He watched the snow drift around the hold in the fence. Soon, not even a wren would be able to get through.

"Why should I bother with her," he thought. "She hates me, and thinks only of her eggs. I can find another bird to nest with me." But in his heart, he knew he would never find another Golden Pheasant. Then, before the hole closed completely, he got up and squeezed through it, back onto the farm.

They talked all night. As the sun sliced the shadows away, Shiela urged, "Run, Herman, while you can."

"No, Shiela. Not without you."

"You must go. I can no longer live the life of freedom. I will stay here, where I am safe."

"Please, Shiela."

"Go now. The goddess is coming soon. Goodbye, Herman. I will always remember what we had."

"Goodbye, Shiela. I love you."

"Goodbye, Herman."

Herman, with feathers drooping, walked back to the hole in the fence, scraped snow away, and slid through. He walked out into the field, now covered with white loneliness.

He never looked back.

Jack Dukes

The Loon & the Tomcat

The yellow tomcat lived all alone on an island in the far north. His tail was twitching as he watched the hatching of a baby bird in the fall coolness.

"What kind of bird am I?" peeped the loon, as he did what no other loon could ever do, and began walking towards the water.

"You're my dinner," thought the tomcat, "as soon as you get a little bigger. I'm going to eat you like I ate your mother, you crazy loon." He watched with slitted, slanted, staring eyes as the loon stumbled through the dry leaves.

"I know I'm a bird, because I came from an egg, but why aren't there any more around like me?"

It stopped, stuck its beak into the air, and sang a song as loud as it could. It listened for an answer, but no answer came, not even an echo. The only sound was leaves rustling under the twitching tail of the tomcat. The bird heard it. It turned around completely, and waddled straight towards the cat's unblinking eyes.

"Hello, mother," it peeped.

"Mother?"

"Yes. The first creature I see after I'm hatched is my mother. I don't know why, but it is so. You're my mother now."

The cat rolled over on his back to play with a catnip plant. "Beat it, kid. You're crazy. It's a good thing I just filled up on mice, or I'd eat you right now."

The cat rolled back into his legs as the bird started to push against his fur. "Cut it out! I'm not your mother. I'm a cat. You're some kind of duck. I never saw a bird quite like you. 'Course, I never saw a baby bird before either. What are you, anyway?"

"I guess I'm a cat, then. Maybe a cat-duck?"

The old tom slashed out a paw, pinned the baby loon to the ground, and hissed right into its face. "Listen, you! I said you're a duck. You're just too dumb. I ought to eat you right now."

But he was only playing a cruel cat game, and he let the baby bird go.

"What kind of food do you eat, duck?"

"Fish. Plants too, I think."

"Fish! Now you're talking my language. Tell you what, kid. I'll be your mother if you'll bring me fish. OK?"

"Thank you, mother. I'll bring you the best fish in the river."

A month went by. They got along together very well. The duck followed the cat everywhere, and, though it had no claws or fangs, it learned the value of stealth, patience, and ambush. They worked very well, especially in underwater fishing. Instead of swimming into a school of fish, and catching one by chance, it learned to pick out the best fish, wait for it to get full and lazy, and then dive after it. It kept the cat happy, and that's all the loon knew to care about, until the fifth week, when snow buried the island in white silence.

The duck walked into the water, and then through the shallows until it could paddle. It paddled so hard that it almost ran on the surface of the water. It ran with the current, then against the current; into the wind and away from the wind. It ran until it barely had strength enough to get back to shore. As soon as it caught its breath, it walked straight up to the tomcat.

"I want to fly, mother."

"I was watching your crazy shenanigans. You'd be best off saving your energy for fishing. If I get too hungry, I'll eat you. Besides, you can't fly. You have no wings."

"I don't believe you, mother. I can too fly."

The duck stuck its head into the air and sang its song louder than it ever had before.

"Look, kid, I'm sorry, but you were born out of season. You're a defective. You've got no wings. You'll never learn to fly. Give up. Go get me a fish, or take up mousing. When are you ever going to learn?"

"I'm sorry, mother. I have to try."

The duck tried all winter, but never learned to fly. It got very good at walking though, even though loons aren't supposed to walk. It even learned to run. It had to learn to run, because the cat chased it whenever he was bored, or restless. The duck got to rest only when the cat was lazy from being full of fish.

When spring came, the duck was happy that winter was over. Birds came back in flocks and filled the air with songs of every sort. The duck watching every one, and sang to those that came close enough to hear.

"Am I a bird like you?"

No bird stopped even to answer as they flew on by. One day, the duck stuck its head up to the sky and screamed, "What kind of bird am I? Why can't I fly?"

One by one, they swooped down to look the duck over, but because the cat was there, none of them would land. "No," they said, one after another as they soared away. Owls, crows, gulls, and herons: all disowned the duck. But still, it practiced trying to fly and brought the cat fresh fish every day.

Before the spring was over, the cat stopped purring over the fish. The duck became afraid that it was not pleasing the cat, and tried even harder to bring him better fish. It was afraid of being eaten, because the cat never let it forget that that was the punishment for failure. The summer was hot, but the duck never stopped working. The cat was just lying in the sun and getting fat. The duck grew strong by trying to fly. It practiced its song every day, always hoping for an answer, but never getting one.

Fall came again, and the air was full of the thunder of hunter's guns. One hunter built a blind on the edge of the mainland, just across the channel of the island. He shot at every duck that flew near. Twice, wounded ducks fell on the island. The loon rushed to try and find them, but the cat got to them first, and ate them. Then, a wounded mallard fell into the big slough that made up the center of the island.

"Dinner!" meowed the cat, and because he was so fat with food that he didn't even have to exercise to get, he walked slowly towards it, pausing to sniff at everything of interest along the way.

"A duck!" laughed the duck, and set off as swiftly as its legs would carry it.

The cat and the duck reached the slough at the same time. The mallard had managed to land in the middle of the slough. It was there now, its wings tipped beneath the surface of the water as if held there by something unseen.

"Bring me that bird, duck!" commanded the cat. "I don't want to get my paws wet."

"No, mother. I want to talk to it first. Maybe it can tell me what kind of bird I am. Can you, noble duck?"

"Not if you give me to that cat!"

"I won't. I promise that the cat can't have you. Do you know what kind of bird I am?"

"Not exactly. I saw one like you once. It was a loon. I remember that it had a beautiful song."

"Like this?" The loon stuck its head up into the air and sang as loud and pure as it could.

"That's close, but the other song was much prettier."

"Can I fly?"

"I really don't know. I don't really care. I'm dying, you know. The mallard's head dipped into the water as he tried to scare away the minnows that were already gathering beneath him. He kept his head under for so long that the loon became afraid. He poked the mallard's neck and tried to lift his head up.

"Please don't die yet. If you do, I'll let that cat get you. I need to know if I can fly."

The mallard lifted his head, but his neck was weak, and it swayed his head back and forth, and side to side. "You're a silly bird. Of course you can fly. You have wings, don't you?"

"No."

The mallard got angry. "I can see them with my own eyes."

"Then why can't I fly?"

The mallard's bill splashed into the water. The loon swan under his neck, and head his head onto its back until his strength was built back up.

"Let's see you flap your wings."

"I can't."

"Of course you can, you silly bird, if you'll just let me have my head back."

The loon swam out from under his head.

"What do you mean, you can't flap your wings. Show them to me. Well, I'll be a decoy. They're fastened together at the tips. I'll bet that you were a late baby."

"That's what mother said."

"Where's mother? Maybe she can help me."

"That's her...the cat."

The mallard flopped his head around and stared at the cat standing right at the water's edge.

"Wow! Kid, I don't have enough time left to tell you...to tell you...about the bird I saw...I saw that looked like...looked like you." The mallard's head moved in figure eights. "That cat....that cat isn't your mother. You have to find a way...find a way to get your wingtips...wingtips free. I think I'm going to die now. Goodbye, goodbye."

"Please don't die, Mr. Mallard. I've waited all my life to talk to another duck. Don't leave me now."

But the mallard's head drooped all the way under the water, and stayed there. Nothing that the loon could do made any difference. A bubble of air left the mallard's nostrils and popped in the crispness of the autumn air.

"Bring me that bird!"

The tomcat's tail slashed the air with every word. The loon jumped at the screech in his voice.

"No. I promised I wouldn't let you have him."

"Stupid kid! The crayfish and crows will be eating him next. You bring me that bird, or I'm making you my next dinner."

"No, I won't! You lied to me. You said I didn't have wings."

"Well, you might as well not have them. You and your dumb running. Loons aren't supposed to walk, you know, let alone run. You bring me that bird before I come after you both."

"No! No! No! I made a promise."

The cat crouched and spring into the water with a terrible hiss. The loon swam to meet it head on. Only twenty-five feet separated them, and it closed rapidly.

"OK, smart guy. You're my dinner tonight."

"Guy? Am I a guy bird?"

"Sure. Didn't you ever look at yourself in the river?"

The cat took a swipe at the tail feathers of the loon, but it dove under, and came up on the other side of the cat.

"Why did you make me keep running, when you knew I had wings?"

"To make your legs strong for swimming, so I got the best fish."

The loon pushed hard with both legs. The shove sent him scooting through the water so fast that he left a wake. He gave another shove and floated in front of the cat, just out of range of his claws. "Thank you, mother."

The cat's voice softened. "Look, kid, I'm tired and want to get to shore. Just bring me that bird, and we'll forget all about this."

"Dog nightmares to you!"

The cat shrieked. "You just wait until you come back to shore, you smart-mouthed bird! You've had your last chance." The cat swam away, got back onto dry land, and sat there, licking his fur, waiting.

The duck swam for hours, but the cat never stopped watching. When dusk drew near, the loon turned his beak up to the sky, and sang more powerfully than ever before. Then, he turned and headed straight for those slitted, slanted, staring eyes. The tomcat jerked into a half-crouch, hissing a deadly warning. The duck swan straight on, until, halfway, he dove beneath the waters. But the cat's eyes never left the tattle-tale ripples on the surface. Three times, the loon came up at different spots, only to find the cat in his way.

"Get out of my way, mother cat, or I'll stab you like I do a fish."

Straight at the cat the loon swam. The tomcat leaped into the water almost on top of him. He lifted a paw and slashed it like a four-bladed axe at the duck's back. The loon sank just deep enough into the water to let the claws slide through his feathers. One claw caught exactly in the skin that held the wingtips together. The cat growled in triumph as he opened his mouth to bite the loon to death. The loon stuck his head up in the air, and sang his own song of combat as mightily as he could. Then, he began swimming in giant circles, around and around. His powerful legs carried him so fast that the cat was drowned in his wake.

The loon was tired and wanted to rest. He tried to wade onto shore, but the claw was firmly stuck, and he couldn't drag the waterlogged cat out of the water. Back out to the mallard he swam.

It was hard to do, because the cat was sinking. The loon was very tired.

"Mr. Mallard, I wish you had not died. You could tell me what to do. All you left me was your words, 'You have to find a way to get your wingtips free.' I thought I had, but it did not work. Now, you are dead, the cat is dead, and I wish I were dead too."

The cat was sinking deeper even as the loon was speaking, and soon pulled the loon under the water with him. The loon caught and ate two of the fish that were nibbling at the mallard's feet. It gave him strength, but not right away. Down and down they sank, until all the light disappeared. The loon could not even see the end of his beak. In the blackness of the bottom, he could not even see which way to go. Indeed, once his feet left the bottom, he was not even sure of which way was up.

"It sure is nice down here," said the loon. The loon was getting silly from holding his breath too long. "If I just gave up and stayed here, maybe that would be the best thing to do. I don't want to live all alone."

Just then, the loon bumped into a giant cottonwood tree that had long ago blown down. Its trunk slanted upwards towards the surface and the light. "No," he though. "I have to find out what a loon is. I have to keep trying." He began climbing the trunk of the tree, dragging the cat behind him.

Twice, the cat's body got stuck in branches. Each time, the loon wanted to quit, but he kept climbing anyway. He tugged and hauled until the branches broke free. Up and up he climbed until, finally, his beak and eyes were out of the water. But he could go no further. The cat, again, was firmly stuck. Tug as he would, he could not free it. He stuck his beak straight up at the sky, took a huge breath, and sang his song differently than he ever had before. With his cry filling the air, he made a desperate lunge for the top. This time, the branch did not break. But the cat's body tore free anyway, and remained behind in the crotch of the cottonwood. He walked onto shore, never even knowing that the cat's claw had torn through the skin that had held his wingtips together.

"I have to rest now," he said, and walked back to the tree where his egg had been hatched. "The mallard's crow friends will eat him, and that's OK. The cat ate the fish, and now the fish will eat the cat, and that's OK. I know that I'm a loon, but I don't know what a loon is. I know I'm supposed to fly, but I can't use my wings. I can walk and run, but loon's aren't supposed to do that. And I'm all alone. I'm the unhappiest bird in the whole world."

He walked down into the hollow at the base of the tree where he had been hatched. As he gave a mighty yawn, his wings stretched out almost to their full span and he saw their full beauty for the first time.

"My wings! They're free! I can fly!"

His tiredness was forgotten as he ran out into the water and flapped his wings over and over. Their muscles were weak from non-use, but he wanted to fly so badly that not even that would stop him. He stuck his beak up into the air, and sang his song the loudest and purest of his whole life. His wingtips beat against the wake his breast made, leaving a trail of tiny whirlpools on both sides. His feet beat faster and faster until he was practically running on the surface. Against he sang his song, and ran even faster. Then, not even the loon's feet were touching. Neither were his wingtips. He flew upward at a slant, like he was going up a ramp, until he was above the treetops, and saw the world as he had never known it to be. He saw birds in the sky around him: geese and mallards and pelicans. He stuck his beak straight out in front of him, and sang a song different than he had ever sung before. It made every bird look at him. Even a bird so far away as to be a speck heard his cry and changed her course to intercept with his.

"Why, you look like me!" he said. "Are you a loon?"

"Of course I'm a loon. Didn't I answer your mating call?"

"What is a loon?"

"Lord, help me. Were you a late baby, by any chance?"

"That's what mother cat said."

"Mother cat? This is going to be tougher than I thought. Well, a loon…"

The Red-Tailed Hawks

Near the edge of the forest, where a deep ravine made a crooked slash through the canopy of trees, a fox sniffed its way along an accustomed trail, sniffing the strange odor of the trapper who had been along the trail the day before. Above, a red-tailed hawk loafed on quiet wings against the clean, blue skies of October. Both of them sensed the meat at the same time. The hawk, with eyes eight times as keen as human eyes, set his wings at just the right angle to stall into a power-dive. The fox, nose full of the promise of a meal, broke into a trot as the odor grew stronger. The hawk's talons slashed at the meat. He missed, and almost crashed into the small shrubbery that supported it. As he flared off, and started climbing for another pass, the fox reached the meat. More cautious, because of the strong smell of the trapper, the fox sniffed the area before entering it. Just as she reached for it with brilliant teeth, the hawk smashed into it with the talons of both legs, and jerked it right out of the fox' mouth. A snare, meant for the fox, sawed itself around the right wing of the hawk and jerked him out of the air. The meat, thrown free when the hawk's body whipped around, landed just at the feet of the fleeing fox, who took it and ran swiftly away.

    The hawk fought furiously against the wire that bound it, but talons and a beak was no match. He only succeeding in slashing through his own skin until nerves and ligaments were completely severed. He kept it up until there was no more pain and no more energy. When the trapper came by, the hawk seemed dead. "Poor bird," he said, and threw its body into the shallow stream at the end of the ravine.

The cooling waters slowly revived him, and then washed away the fevers of his recovery. An abundance of curious minnows gave him food. He lay quietly for several days, until his wing had healed and the pain gone away. Then, he tried to fly. He could not. His rage was fierce as he screamed at the world around him.

"What good am I now? It was all my fault, too. I should have known better. Too bad I didn't die. I should have died. I'm just too simple-minded to live. From now on, that's what I'll call myself...Mr. Simple."

In the grasses of the swampland nearby, he spotted an old, dead pine tree. He found a hollow in its base that suited him perfectly for a nest.

At first, he tried to catch his food by running on the ground like a chicken, but he caught only an occasional toad. His talons were forever getting caught in the tangled brush and weeds. This day, he managed to free himself in time to catch a large, fat toad just before it could jump into the water.

"Hello there." The pleasant voice came from a small tree just at his side. "That's a very nice toad you caught."

Mr. Simple was startled, not just at her voice, but at her words too, for no one had ever told him before that a toad was nice.

"Don't be silly," he replied. "Toads aren't nice. But they're practically all that I have to eat. I have been badly wounded, and wish I were dead."

"I certainly can't understand why," she said. "I watched you catch the toad. You were very patient in freeing your talons from the grass and strong in the way you hopped up to it. I don't think you are badly wounded. Why, I'll bet that if you used your good wing, you could hop right over these weeds, and even catch a rabbit! Well…maybe a young rabbit."

Mr. Simple was shocked at her suggestion. What a stupid little bird, he thought. Doesn't she know that if that were possible to do, I would already be doing it? "You are kind with your words," he said, "but I will show you that it is quite impossible."

He smashed his good wing towards the ground as if an enemy were under it. It lifted him a full inch. She cheered. He smiled and smashed his wing down over and over, smiling and chuckling as his head popped up and down all around the base of the tree that she sat in, sometimes only an inch, sometimes three or four.

While he was practicing, she flew off, back to her nest, but she returned to visit him almost every day. Soon, she was telling him of all the troubles of her nest: about how Filbert, her mate, called her bad and told her she was a poor nestkeeper, and knew next to nothing about rearing fledglings.

Mr. Simple's heart responded. "Though you may have no value in his eyes, you are the most valuable hawk in the world to me. If Filbert is your broken wing, then you must do as you taught me to do, and use your good wing to jump over the weeds. Come with me. I have something to show you."

Clooney followed him into his nest, which connected to a small work room right in the trunk of the pine.

"See?" he said, "I may yet fly! I've been working on a new wing. Of course, it doesn't work yet, but the more times I build it, the more I understand about it. One day, it will do what I want it to do."

"Mr. Simple, that's terrific! I'm so excited! I just know that you'll be able to fly again."

"Thank you, Clooney. You are the best friend I've ever had."

"You are my best friend too, Mr. Simple. I wish...oh, never mind." She touched his feathers briefly, and left without another word.

Mr. Simple was inspired by her approval and worked harder than ever on his wing. *If only I could fly again, I could bring her better food than that simpleton mate of hers,* he thought. He toiled day and night to make it so, but nothing worked.

One day, when he was tired and discouraged from yet another failure, Clooney touched his feathers. Always before, she had moved away when their feathers touched, but this time, she let the touch remain.

"Mr. Simple," she said, "I love you."

"I love you too, Clooney."

He moved closer to her until they both could feel the warmth of each other's bodies. They began clacking bills and continued until all their troubles were forgotten and nothing mattered but them.

****

Clooney didn't see Mr. Simple for a while after that. He didn't mind. The memory of her last visit was enough to make him happy as he worked on, learning by trial and error. As his knowledge of what would not work grew, his vision of what might work changed, until, one day, he flew. It wasn't far, fast, or high, but it was real.

"I did it! I did it! I did it!" He shouted at the trees, for no one was around to share his happiness. It was on that very day that Clooney returned.

"Why, hello Clooney! How fortunate that you are here! I have just this day flown above the tree tops with my newest wing."

She didn't respond.

"What's the matter, Clooney? Aren't you happy for me?"

"Of course I am, Mr. Simple. It's just that I'm so mad at Filbert. He doesn't come home anymore, until he's too tired to clack bills. I've decided not to nest with him any longer."

Mr. Simple wasted no time. "Come on inside, Clooney!"

Clooney didn't waste any time, either.

"Ohhhh, Mr. Simple!"

"Ohhhh, Clooney!"

She didn't leave until she was sure that Filbert ought to be asleep. Before she flew away, she touched Mr. Simple and said, "No one has ever done for me what you have done, Mr. Simple."

"I hope I didn't offend you, Clooney."

"Oh no, Mr. Simple, you didn't! I loved every second of it. I want all of it I can get." And she flew away.

****

Mrs. Barely came calling on Mr. Simple soon after.

"Hello Mr. Simple. I'm Mrs. Barley. Clooney told me all about you. I told her I would like to meet you myself, so she asked me to bring you a message...she doesn't want to see you anymore."

Mr. Simple was crushed. Mrs. Barley comforted him by moving in with him and clacking bills both day and night. Mr. Simple only got worse. He stopped working on his wing and just stayed around his nest, getting in her way. She grew tired of his grumpiness, and flew back to her old nest. She told her troubles to a neighbor. His mate had flown away in the middle of the nesting season, and he found it difficult to care for his fledglings alone.

"What a rascal of a bird that Mr. Simple is," he said, and seemed accidentally to touch her tail feathers. Soon, she moved out of Mr. Simple's nest and into her neighbors. Mr. Simple shuddered and slowly resumed his normal activities.

****

On another day, while searching for a nest near better hunting grounds, he stumbled across a meadow bordered by tall pines on one side, and a river on the other. Hawks lived here too, but they were not Red-tails – they were Ospreys. He had hopped only a few feet into the clearing when one of them sailed down to meet him.

"Hello," she sang. "I see that you have been wounded. Won't you tell me about yourself? I'm Agatha."

"Why, hello Agatha," he stammered. "I'm Mr. Simple, and I'm looking for a better nest."

"Ohhhh," she said. "You have come to just the right place. I have a tree that's much too big for me. I see that your wing is no good any longer. No matter. I catch plenty of food. I would be very happy to share it with you."

"No, thank you. This is truly a beautiful spot, and your offer is kind, but I am not like you. We cannot share the same nest, or even the same tree. Once, I could fly with your kind, but no more. They would laugh at even my best efforts, for I cannot yet fly in a straight line. They would call me a butterfly."

"But they scorn me too. I once took a Cooper's Hawk to mate. They said I was bad. But I can fly as well as even the bachelor birds, although I am past nesting age."

"A Cooper's Hawk? You certainly are brave. What happened?"

"He just played all the time. I brought him the finest food I could find, but it was never good enough for him. I made him leave."

"That's interesting, Agatha, but I see a storm approaching. I must return at once. Goodbye." He began hopping away.

"Wait!" hollered Agatha. "Won't you tell me where you live? I'll come to visit you."

"At the base of the tall, dead pine at the edge of the swamp. I will be happy to welcome you!"

The clouds seemed to be moving faster, so Mr. Simple began using his wing to get bigger hops. Lightning flashed. Thunder answered at once. Huge drops began beating on his feathers. By the time he reached the area his tree was in, the storm was directly overhead. It was raining so hard that he could barely see. Then, when he was only a few trees away, a bolt struck his tree, splitting it from top to bottom and setting it afire near the top.

Mr. Simple, afraid for his nest, rushed to see in spite of the flames that rapidly burned through the rotten core towards his nest, which was now open to the rain. He managed to save the best one of the wings he'd built, but even it was charred. He dragged it over to a small cave in the roots of another tree, and stayed awake all night, although the storm moved out as swiftly as it had come in.

The next morning, as soon as the sun came up into a sky of total blue, he went to see if anything else could be salvaged. There was nothing. He quit poking in the mud made by ashes and rain, and stood looking at his former home. All of his feathers pointed to the ground. He didn't notice the speck in the sky, growing larger and larger until Agatha landed right beside him. He didn't even look up as she spoke.

"I'm so sorry, Mr. Simple. Was this your nest?"

"Yes," he said in a soft voice. "It was also my workshop. I was building a new wing for myself. Now it is gone, all gone."

"Do you have someplace to go?"

"No. This was all I had."

"You must come with me, then. My nest is large. There is room enough for both of us."

"No, thank you. Well...I don't know. Maybe I should. But only for a little while. Just until I can find a new nesting tree."

"Fine," she agreed. "Then come along now. The sooner you are away from here, the sooner you will be better. Shall I carry your imitation wing?"

Mr. Simple looked at her for the first time. "Imitation? That is not imitation. That is real. With it, I can fly. Not so well as I once could, but well enough to catch any mouse in the swamp."

"Oops," she said softly. "It's a very nice wing. Will you put it on and fly back with me? I would enjoy seeing you fly."

"I supposed I might as well. There's nothing left for me here."

He donned his wing, took three fast hops, and began to fly. Agatha, though she could fly faster and higher, matched her speed to his and never once mentioned her superiority. She told him how clever he was, and how proud she was to be flying beside him.

"It feels different," he said. "The fire did something to it."

Before she could answer, they were at her nest. It was a huge one, but it was not until they were in it that he realized what a big bird she was. She could easily step up to the edge of it, while he had to hop up to it in two steps. He found a nook for himself and a cranny for his wing. He stayed awake all night, wondering why loudly snoring birds hadn't been eliminated by patrolling pterodactyls a long time ago.

Three days later, after nibbling away at the charred part of his wing, he donned it for a trial fly. He rose into the sky until he was but a pin-speck. Then, he dove towards the nest where she sat preening. She watched him do roller coasters and figure eights as he approached. Finally, he landed beside her, every feather aquiver with exhilaration.

"The fire did what I could not do. I thought I needed a large, heavy wing, but the fire made it shorter and trimmed down the edge. Wasn't that a lucky fire? It gave me a new wing."

"Well, yes, I suppose it was, Mr. Simple. I'm so very pleased that something good came out of the fire." But her feathers, in spite of her care, showed that she was not pleased at all. Mr. Simple was too excited to notice.

"I've decided to go away and find another nest," he chattered. "There's forest I've heard about that I've always wanted to see. The water never turns hard there, and mice play in the grasses all year round."

"I think I've had enough sun," said Agatha, and she turned to step down into her nest. He followed.

"What's wrong, Agatha?"

"You haven't clacked bills with me since you came here. You tell me about clacking bills with everyone else. Why not me?"

"But Agatha, I don't feel that way about you."

Her feathers drooped for a second. "I understand," she said, "but will you respect the feelings I have for you?"

"Of course, Agatha. You are my friend."

"I love you, Mr. Simple."

"Oh, my goodness," said Mr. Simple, and flew off to find a new workshop. The next day, Agatha got a message that made her fly away.

"I don't know when I can be back," she said. "My brother has had an emergency. Please treat my nest as your own. Goodbye."

"Goodbye, Agatha. Please take my good wishes with you."

Three days later, Mr. Simple realized how nice it was to have her around. "I must find something to do," he twitted, and flew off to see his old home. As he neared, he spotted another Red-tailed Hawk on the ground next to the burnt out base.

Those tail-feathers look familiar, he though, and came down on the sunny side for a better look. She spotted him about the same time he recognized her.

"Mr. Simple!" she shrieked. "You're alive!"

"Of course I'm alive, Mrs. Barely," he frowned. "I wouldn't be here if I weren't, would I? Whatever are you doing here?"

"Why, looking for you, of course. Clooney asked about you last week, and I didn't know, so I came to see for myself, and ohhh, Mr. Simple, I'm so glad to see you and know that you're alright!"

She hopped over to him and began rubbing his tail-feathers quite happily. Mr. Simple responded at once, and they began clacking bills as if no time had passed between them.

"My goodness," said Mr. Simple afterwards. "I didn't realize how much I'd missed you."

"What?" asked Mrs. Barely.

"I said, I thought you had a nest-mate. Did something happen?"

"Oh, no. He's still there. But he isn't very exciting. I thought that you wouldn't mind seeing me again."

"Mind! Goodness, no! How is Clooney?"

"She misses you very much. So do I. Where are you staying now?"

"With an Osprey named Agatha. She's bigger than I am by half. She has a huge nest with lots of room for me. And I have a new workshop not far from there. Right now, she's away to Frog Willow Marsh. Her brother got shot by a hunter. I miss her."

"I'm sorry, Mr. Simple, but I must go. My mate is due back soon. I don't want him to know I've been gone."

"Dear me," said Mr. Simple. "Well, goodbye. I hope we meet again."

"No. We never will. I was wrong." And off she flew without a single turn of her head. "Gooodddbbyyeeee," streamed behind her. "IIII Illoooovvve yyyoooouuuuu."

Three days later, Agatha was still away. Mr. Simple was so intent on hustling about his old nest that he didn't see a speck in the sky growing as it headed straight for him. Then, very faintly, he heard his name being called. The sound became clearer and clearer, until he could focus on it easily. His body knew before his mind did. His tail feathers stiffened and grew even redder. "Clooney!" he screamed, and flew up to meet her.

In mid-air, they wheeled and dove, taking turns in the lead, sending shrieks of sheer happiness into the forest below. Clooney suddenly dove into the treetops, with Mr. Simple in hot pursuit. Twisting and dodging through branches, she headed back to his old home. As they neared it, he raced ahead, and landed on the ground to await her.

"Welcome, Clooney!" he said, and she lit down just in front of him.

"I love you, Mr. Simple."

"I love you too, Clooney," he answered, and without further words, they began clacking bills. They didn't stop until the sun had set and the moon had run the full length of the sky. They rubbed tail-feathers one last time before they left, promising to meet in three days so that they could spend some daylight hours together.

Agatha was waiting for him.

"Why, hello Agatha! Welcome back!"

She pressed up against him and began rubbing feathers. "My brother's wings are shattered. He will never fly again."

"Oh my goodness," he said, and lost his balance sideways. She covered him immediately and began clacking bills without another word.

Mr. Simple couldn't respond.

"Where have you been?" she asked sweetly as she crawled off of him.

"With Clooney."

"Who else did you see when I was gone?"

"Mrs. Barely."

"I thought she was nesting with a mate now."

"She is, but he, like Clooney's mate, fails to satisfy her hungers."

"Do they satisfy yours?"

"Yes. Each in different ways."

Agatha turned to face him beak-to-beak. "Will you give them up and become my mate and nest with me? I love you, you know."

"Dear me, no," he said, and moved to the edge of the nest. "I was mated once. When my wing was ruined, she flew away. Now I see how unhappy Clooney and Mrs. Barely are, and that makes me afraid. I don't think that mating is such a good idea."

"I am different."

"Clooney also wants me to mate with her."

"That isn't so."

Mr. Simple hopped back so that he could face her. "What do you mean?" he demanded.

"Where is she now?"

"In her nest," mumbled Mr. Simple, "with her mate."

"Go to sleep now and get your rest. I am with you, and my love for you is whole."

"My love for you is not."

"I know. But a wise bird mates with one who loves him, not with the one he loves. Go to sleep now."

"Yes. My head is very tired."

Agatha awoke Mr. Simple by stroking his tail-feathers. The sun sent warmth creeping into the nest, while the breeze brought back aromas of food-filled lands. Mr. Simple stretched, blinked at the cloudless sky, and started returning her strokes. She stopped him.

"Don't," she whispered. "Just let me love you."

Mr. Simple did. Later, he said "Agatha, you are a great bird, in more than just size. Perhaps I will be your mate, but I must see Clooney again first." And off he flew.

He spiraled into the sky until not even Agatha could see him. Then, he flew straight to Clooney's nest. He dove silently into it, hoping to surprise her. She was not there. Up again he spiraled, feeling power and pride in his wooden wing. When he was high enough to scan the land, her saw her at the edge of the swamp. She and Filbert were laughing as they taught their young ones to hunt. He flew back to his burnt-out tree to wait.

When she came to keep their appointment, she rushed up to him, stroked his feathers, and said "I love you, Mr. Simple."

"I love you too, Clooney, but I must let you go."

Clooney's feathers drooped so that they seemed to touch the forest floor. "Why, Mr. Simple?"

"You have a mate. You work with him and play with him, and train your young together."

"But I do not love him."

"It is not necessary that you love him. It is only necessary that you be loyal, as I will be to Agatha. Perhaps you will learn to love him in a different way, as I might Agatha. Goodbye, Clooney. Watch me fly with my new wing. Without you, I might never have made it work."

He launched himself into the air, and flew every acrobatic trick he could recall. Then, he flew patterns that only he could fly.

"See, Clooney? You gave me back my will to fly. Now I must go and build wings for others. Your gift will be given many times."

He spoke to her on the wing, and slowly, her feathers picked themselves up. Suddenly, she flew up to meet him. Together, they wheeled, climbed, dove, and soared as if the sky was theirs alone. Then, as high as they could possibly climb, they met and locked together. Spinning downwards at first, in full, lazy circles, they clacked bills. Lost in each other, they started falling faster and faster until, just above the treetops, they broke apart.

"Goodbye, Clooney. I must go now."

"Goodbye, Mr. Simple. I will love you forever."

Clooney headed back to her nest, flying slowly, just above the trees. Mr. Simple flew swiftly and surely, headed for his new workshop. Neither one looked back.

Under a Hunter's Moon

The steel jaws of the leg trap snapped shut across the right front paw of the red fox as she loped along her favorite trail through the frozen bluffs of the Mississippi River in the middle of Minnesota. It was like catching a human hand across the palm. In her fight for freedom, she broke her paw bones, and cut the flesh half through. There was no blood. The pressure of the jaws had instantly sealed broken vessels.

She struggled for half-a-mile, zigzagging between twin snowmobile tracks, dragging the trap's six-foot-long anchor branch behind her. Tracks in the two inches of fresh snow that fell the night before clearly showed where she left the open and entered the woods atop a bluff that fell 150 feet straight down to a river of ice.

Trapper hadn't believed that he would catch a fox that morning, so he was careless and left behind the claw hammer that would have knocked the fox out. He could then kill it by stepping on its chest, crushing its heart and lungs while preserving the integrity of the hide.

"Hot damn! I got me one! Hope it's not a damned gray."

He walked as fast as his bad leg would allow, but he needn't have worried. The trap's drag had caught in bramble bushes, and the fox was pinned. It was a red female, almost orange, with black paws and ears.

"Hot damn! That's eighty-five bucks!"

He broke off a four-foot length of a rotten oak branch to club her to unconsciousness. She snarled as he approached. Her jaws were bleeding from biting everything around her. Red-spotted bark and snow told the silent story of her struggle. At arm's length, he swung. The club was too rotten to do the job, and broke in half as it hit her skull. She counterattacked with a lunge that gave her freedom, but left half a paw in the trap. Her teeth ripped off the little finger of his left hand as she headed for the edge of the bluff.

"You rotten cur!"

He half ran, half stumbled through the snow after her, still carrying the two-foot stub of oak branch. Just as the fox reached the edge, he threw the club with all his might. It hit her in her side, and knocked her over the rim. He reached the rim in time to see her running flat out on the snow-covered river ice. He stood there, cursing, vowing revenge as his own blood mingled in the snow with the blood of the fox.

Revenge didn't come easy. The fox seemed to know every trick that Trapper knew. Even the animals of the woods appeared to cooperate to frustrate him. Owls and hawks sailed down to steal the rabbit heads and muskrat carcasses that were intended to lure the fox to the leg traps buried beneath the snow. Rabbits and abandoned cats pushed aside the neck snares concealed along the favorite runways of the fox population. Mice burrowed under the hidden, steel-jawed traps to steal the scent-soaked cotton, and left it lying on top of the trap to warn the foxes away.

The doctor didn't help matters any when, two days later, Trapper went to get his infected wound tended.

"I want you to start a series of rabies shots right away. I can have the vaccine here this afternoon."

"You're out of your mind! If I ain't gonna let you give me no human blood, I sure as hell ain't gonna let you stick me with no needle full of sheep brains."

"You've got no choice, Trapper, and frankly, I'm glad. Maybe a taste of pain will burn out some of the hate in your head."

"I got a choice, Doc. A man's always got a choice." His voice emphasized *man*. "Don't go ordering none of that stuff for me. I'll get that dirty pup, and drop her off right here in your lap."

"She has to be alive. That means you can't use any of those neck snares that you're so fond of. And you have to start injections no later than the seventh day. Two-and-a-half days are already gone."

Trapper started to walk out while the doctor was still talking. He stopped as he reached for the doorknob. His bandage contrasted oddly with his tanned and heavy hand. It made the practical grunginess of his outdoor clothing seem dirty. The doctor went on, his voice raised a little.

"I don't like what you do, Trapper. Part of me hopes you fail. I think I'd enjoy giving you the rabies shots. They set your guts on fire."

"You just get a pen ready, Doc. But I want her back when you're done with her. Just remember that the 85 bucks her hide brings is what's going to pay your bill."

He left without another word.

For two more days, he tried with all the cunning forty years of trapping had given him. He set traps on each side of the snares so, if the fox tried to go around, she would step into disaster. He used every kind of scent that he could buy, and made up fresh scents from the glands of previously killed animals. He tended the traps twice daily. On the morning of the fifth day, his worry touched the edge of fear. A three-and-a-half pawed trail neatly followed in his own tracks of the day before.

He bought new traps to set in his own footsteps. He boiled them and handled them with gloves fashioned out of fox fur to keep human scent away. The fox still followed, yet at every footstep that held a trap, her path showed that she had either jumped over it, or gone around it. When he set a circle of traps around his trail, she stopped and refused to enter the deadly area. It was as if the fox were watching and remembering everything he did.

By the middle of the sixth day, his frustration had become a deep anger. Seldom in his life had he failed to get what he went after. He was needled in the small-town café, pressed by his doctor, urged to give up by his wife. Instead, though the temperature was forecast for twenty below zero, he announced his plan to walk the fox down. He would follow her trail relentlessly until she was exhausted and could run no further. It was the only way left, but it meant walking in places where four-footed animals could go with ease, and where man might find it impossible to proceed.

He hurried home, changed clothes, and started out at once, carrying only a knife, emergency food rations, a twenty-five-feet coil of barbed wire, and a six-foot walking staff. He picked up her trail easily and followed it into woodlands that stretched for miles on both sides of the river. Only a few scattered, closed-up cabins showed any signs that human beings have ever been there.

He followed the trail until nightfall without sighting her. He took refuge in a cabin by breaking into it. He had forgotten matches, so he ate half his food rations cold and slept on the floor without removing his clothes. When he awoke, he found the rest of his food partially eaten and partially defiled by mice. Instead of opening the door with his hands, he kicked it open, and roaring in rage, threw the remainder of his rations as far as he could.

The cold spell hit with a stunning fury, although the air was clear with arctic purity. The sun was neutralized by winds gusting in the 40's. It was a blizzard without snow. That's when the fox doubled back...into the wind. Lope and rest, lope and rest, but never once letting Trapper rest.

"You dirty pup! Wait'll I get my hands on your hide. I'm gonna stuff it and put it right over my fireplace so's I can remember how you tried to freeze me out. It ain't agonna work, you furry bitch. I ain't got your kind of fur, but I'm a man, by God, and I got me a man's finest cloth to keep me warm."

The fox was a hundred and fifty yards away, sitting in the snow like a calendar picture, watching him bow before the wind as if before an ancient god. They were on the land's edge of the river ice. It was thick enough to support a dozen men, but offered no relief from the wind, which cut into his throat like frozen tacks. On and on she went, a hundred yards at a time. She would sit and wait for him to get so close that he could almost hit her with a snowball. Then, she would lope off to do it all over again.

"You red-coated cur! I wish I had me a gun. Doc or no doc, I'd have you squirting blood like a fire hydrant. You're nothing but a damned animal, killed off our pheasants and spreading your poison around like it was something good."

The fox watched, listened, and then got up and ran off.

"Damn you!"

His shout was torn away by a furious gust that raised a curtain of snow as hard as table salt. When it subsided, the fox was gone.

The bank of the river was three stories high, and as straight up and down as if cut by a cleaver. He hurried to where she had last been. The tracks turned off the ice, led straight to the cliff, and vanished into the windswept limestone dotted with ancient, small caves.

"I gotcha now, you pup! I'll drag you out with my bare hands."

His voice was victorious as he yelled against the wind. He jammed his walking staff viciously into the nearest caves. Each time, he felt the solid thump of rock instead of the yielding flesh of the fox. Again and again he poked until he had searched every cave in reach.

Then he saw it – a crack in the cliff all the way to the top, just big enough for the fox. He backed away to see better, and saw her head looking down, tongue out, triumphant in her ease of escape.

Trapper stood immobile. He stared up at her, panting from his passions, trembling from fighting back the fury that frustration was breeding into him.

"You stay there, damn you. You stay there!"

He turned to retrace his steps a mile and a half, to where he knew he could reach the top. With the wind at his back, he moved as fast as his bad leg would allow, stopping only to catch his breath and let the pain in his leg subside. He kept the pace all the way to where she had last been. There was nothing there but a pile of droppings, already frozen hard. He grasped his staff in both hands and swung at the pile, sending it down to skid on the ice below. He swung at a tree, then a bush, then the ground. He pounded away all around as if the fox might somehow be invisibly there. His finger stump began to bleed through his glove. He took it off, flicked the blood away, and began circling to pick up her trail. A hundred yards away, where a dense bramble thicket had built up a small snow drift, he saw her three and a half footed track. There was an acre of thorns to search. She was nowhere to be seen.

Trapper was hungry and thirsty. He sat down beside her prints, scraped the top layer of snow away, and ate until his thirst was satisfied and his belly numb. He pushed into the thicket for fifty feet. It took ten minutes of crawling, ducking, and using his staff to push the taller branches away. The brush got even thicker, until there was nothing to do but retreat. Back at the starting point, Trapper felt fear boil up from his stomach and spilling into his throat.

"God, why you lettin' this happen? Don'cha care? I'm a man, God, and that's an animal. It ain't right, what's going on. Come on, God, give old Trapper a little help."

Then, he got down on his hands and knees and began crawling around the edge of the patch, searching every bit of snow, every pebble, every leaf for a sign of exit. He circled three fourths of it before seeing where she left the thicket. It was too dark to see where the tracks led. It was too dark to find shelter and too dark to move safely. But the wind had died with the sun. He took refuge in a bathtub sized depression, stripped cedar boughs to cover himself, and, like the animal he sought, curled up to sleep the darkness away.

On the eight day, he awoke before dawn. He was stiff and sore and cold. His leg ached like the muscles were on fire. He began exercising it without getting up. He breathed the sharp air deeply, forcing back the pain, and gradually worked up to a sitting position. As the circulation increased, the aches faded. Finally, he arose and faced the east to let the first rays of sunlight pour heat into his grateful body. Out of modesty's habit, he walked a short way into the thicket to relieve himself. A spot of fur caught his eye, and he saw that the fox had eaten a rabbit. There wasn't much left of it, but he was too hungry to care. He shoved the frozen remains beneath his clothes to thaw them, and ate them raw as soon as they were soft enough to bite.

"Where the hell are you, you dirty pup?"

He roared into the stillness of nothing, and nothing replied.

"Show yourself, damn you! You ain't agonna get away from the Trapper. You can run and hide all you want, but I'll getcha."

A quarter of a mile away, a flock of crows echoed their own curses into the river valley. He grinned and headed in that direction without looking for trail signs. His spirits lifted with the sun, and the gradually increasing ease of walking. He entered a patch of woods so free from underbrush that it looked more like a park than a wilderness. The going was easy, and as he spotted the track near where the crows had guided him, he felt the happiness of confidence return. The fox ran in a straight line through the woods, away from the river. Patches of snow here and there were like road signs.

The woods ended at a clearing. In it was an abandoned, half-destroyed farmhouse. Weeds surrounded it as thickly as bulrushes in a swamp. Beyond it lay a frozen, corn-stubble field.

The fox had circled the clearing at the edge of the woods, and then entered the stubble field. A pile of feathers showed why. She had breakfasted on pheasant, but this time, there was nothing left over. Her tracks then led to the opposite side of the clearing, where she circled around the woods until she entered them again, just a few yards from where she had left them.

Trapper walked back into the woods, out of the woods, and back towards the river. She was loping steadily, increasing the distance between them with every step. He sped up.

"I gotcha now, you red devil. You'll tucker yourself out at this rate. One thing about you damned animals, you ain't got the stamina of a man. I'll run you down, you bloody vixen. I'll run you down and I'll take your hide. Yah. I'll do 'er."

When he reached the bluffs, he saw her far ahead, so far as to seem no bigger than a squirrel. He broke into a trot, and ran until he was puffing.

"Wait a minute, Trapper. There ain't no need to run. You got all day. Just take it easy."

He walked until his breath returned, and then began trotting again. He was winded by the time he reached where she had been. The ground was rough there, covered with stones up to the size of footballs. There was no way to tell which way she had gone. He walked to the edge of the bluff and looked up and down the river for a sign, squinting against the reflected brightness. There was no sign of life of any kind. Not even the crows answered the maddened challenges he hurled into the emptiness.

"Is the fox more valuable to me, God?"

He shook his fist at the sky, which was already clouding over.

"If You ain't gonna help me, leave me alone, damn You!"

It was not so bitter cold as yesterday, but the warmth bred snow into the clouds, until they were swollen, and covered the sky with grey pregnancy. He stood silently for three or four hours, searching with eyes, ears, and instincts. He stood until the snow began falling, and covered the ground with new hope.

"Did you make that snow for me, God? If You did, I'm thanking You for that, Sir."

He moved back from the edge, and then headed downriver, because that's where he would have gone, if he had been the fox. He walked for two hours along the bluff's edge until it became broken with inlets, bays, and backwaters dotted with islands. There was no sign of a track. He walked east for a hundred yards, and retraced his path parallel to the original one. A half hour later, he went back to the edge to scan the river. As he crossed his old trail, he saw her tracks. She had been following him.

"You sneaky bitch! You ain't so damned smart after all. I gotcha now. I got me some good tracking snow."

He turned to follow her trail, so fresh yet that new snow had barely dusted it. She circled, doubled back, and zigzagged. All the while, it kept on snowing. By the time the sun began its descent, every bush was covered, every rock hidden, and each step was a step into the unseen. He plodded along, relying on his staff, oblivious to everything but the trail. Finally, only a few yards away, he saw her. She sat on the near edge of a deep ravine leading to the river. It was as if she waited for him to catch up to her. He ran towards her, staff in front like a raised club. She vanished over the side. As he reached the spot, a rotten log covered with snow gave way beneath his feet. He fell all the way to the bottom, almost unconscious before he reached it.

The fox looked back at him, squatted in the snow, and moved leisurely off upriver on the white-blanketed ice. Her tail was carried high. Her walk, in spite of missing half a paw, seemed proud and dignified. Trapper slipped into darkness. By the time he regained consciousness, he was covered with snow. So were her tracks. Only the depression caused by her urination gave him the clue he needed, but it was enough. By the time night fell, he was back at the bramble thicket, and too exhausted to care. His bed was again the bough-filled depression, and he slept as if dead.

On the morning of the ninth day, he began to go blind. A brilliant, cold sun sent icicle rays into his eyes from the moment he shook off the snow that had enshrouded him during the night. He began the ritual of making his body work. It took longer this morning. Even after he managed to get up, his leg gave way beneath him.

"Damn you, leg!"

He gasped at the pain as he beat on his thigh with the sides of both fists. Don't you do that to me now. Just keep goin' a little while. We'll get her, leg. Come on, damn you.

He sat on the snow, braced backwards against his hands, and crashed his heel over and over into the snow. Finally, his blood began to move again, and freed his muscles from their lip-biting cramps. When he began circling for her trail, he held his staff near his bad leg and sort of hopped a three-tracked trail into four inches of treachery.

He lost count of how many times he stumbled. The vixen's trail ran true parallel to downriver. She crossed through timber and tangle, her stride as constant as a fence row. Even with his circulation restored, he stumbled over weeds and branches which were buried under flat sameness. Only his staff let him make any progress at all. The pain in his eyes became so bad that he kept one eye closed, and the other one slitted enough to barely see through the lashes.

He rested more and more heavily upon his staff, grasping it with both hands, prodding it into the snow ahead of him. Finally, on the near side of a twenty-foot bank, he fell. His staff had slipped off a rock that it was braced against, and threw him off balance. His head struck a stone at the bottom. It stunned him. Each time he snarled his way back from dark sanctuary, his hands clawed the air and his heels dug through snow and frozen leaves until the black earth was bared beneath. When he opened his eyes, everything was blurred. He cuffed his forehead, and shook his head like a dog shaking off water.

"God," he gasped. "I hate You, God."

His voice was quiet, like he was talking to his own hand.

"You and Your damned snow. I can't hate that fox no more. She's better than I am. She's killing me, and You're letting her do it."

He worked his way up to his knees.

"Why don't You kill me, God? 'Stead of letting that fox do it. I never knowed You was real 'til now, but without the fox, there's nothing left to hate but You."

He stood, and his anger made his voice grow stronger.

"I want me that fox, God! You do what You want after that, but I want me that fox. You gimme back my eyes, God!"

His roar rolled into the snow and disappeared.

"Look at what You made me go and do!"

He knelt. The splash of his urine was all that could be heard. He grunted as he made a paste and smeared darkness around his eyes and down the bridge of his nose. He grunted as he arose and crawled his way up the other side of the ravine, feeling the foxes trail with his fingertips. It was too much.

"If You want me dead, kill me now, God. Don't put no more miseries on me. You want me to die of rabies? Foaming at the mouth like a leg-caught coyote? You want that dirty pup to eat me? Maybe before I'm even dead?"

He screamed the next words, into a world as silent as smoke.

"Killll meee, Goddd!"

He crawled beneath a thick pine tree, hid his face on the shaded side of the trunk, and slept until the sun was halfway between noon and darkness. The respite eased his snow-blindness and restored his courage. Nevertheless, he kept his eyes squinted as he hurried along the trail with renewed determination.

When the sun touched the top of the westerly trees, the fox left the woods and began loping along the edge of the river, close to the shore. Trapper was suddenly happy. He could move faster on ice. For a mile and a half, the fox ran true to her course. Then, she veered onto a frozen backwater area that Trapper knew only too well. It was an area of springs that permitted only the thinnest of ice layers to form. It was treacherously pitted with camouflages areas of weakness that would plunge any animal heavier than a fox into several feet of frigid water.

He walked slowly into the backwater, pounding the ice ahead of him with his walking staff. He knew that there was a den at the back end of the slough that the fox could hold up in. Step by step, he moved closer to the shore. He pounded so vigorously with his staff that, when it finally broke through, he lost his balance and fell to the ice with enough force to break it. The water there was only two feet deep, but his awkward position left him soaked to the top of his hips. The water ran inside his clothing. He stood up and walked slowly to shore. He knew he should find shelter before the wetness froze on him, but he went to the cave instead. When he saw her tracks leading to it, he sat down to relish his victory.

"You dirty pup. You got my finger inside your belly, and your poison in my blood, but you ain't gonna kill me. God wouldn't let you do that. You squat in the snow, and every buck that comes along knows you was there and would follow you to their graves...but not me. I'm a man, and you're an animal."

He shrugged the knapsack around to his chest. He took out the coil of barbed wire and let the knapsack slide back. Before undoing the tie on the wire, he laid his staff in easy reach. Then, he began feeding the wire into the cave. He fed it slowly, feeling as he went, and twisted the wire savagely each time it met with the slightest obstruction. Finally, he heard a yelp and a snarl. He grinned and twisted the wire around and around until it could be twisted no more.

Fifteen feet of the wire was in the cave. He began recircling the outstretched strand back onto the coil. Each full circle dragged the fox forward about six inches. He knew there was no escape for her now. There was time to be neat. When only six feet of wire remained to be coiled, he held the coil in his left hand and picked up the staff to use as a club. He pulled back on the coil until the fox' head appeared in the cave's entrance. The wire led beneath its chin and was tangled in the chest and armpit skin. He raised the club, pulled the fox out a little more, and hit her exactly between the eyes.

"Hot damn! That's eight-five bucks and no damn shots!"

He started to get up to tie its feet and muzzle for the long haul back. His lower body wouldn't move. His staff was two feet beyond his reach. He had tossed it, unthinkingly, after its use as a club was done. His clothes were frozen solidly to the ground, and he slowly realized that he had come here to die.

"You dirty pup. You're going to be there to welcome me into hell."

He dragged the fox over to his lap, bent over it with his chest, grasped his legs, and squeezed with all the strength he had left. He wanted to force the air out of the fox' lungs and prevent it from ever breathing again. And that's the position he was in when the rescue party found him that night, under the hunter's moon, half frozen but alive thanks to the body heat of the unconscious fox.

While there was still enough moonlight to see, another muzzle appeared at the mouth of the cave. With tail held high, a fox trotted swiftly off to an upriver trail, leaving behind a clear set of three-and-a-half pawed tracks.

Another Time, Another War, Another Mother

I was sitting on the front porch with Grandpa, watching him spit tobacco juice at the ground wasps as they emerged from their burrows in the grassless front lawn. Our house didn't have any paint neither.

"Here comes your Uncle Carroll now," he said.

Carroll was blond, lean, strong-muscled, 20 years old, and Grandma's love and joy. She worshipped him with all the adoration her Cherokee heritage demanded.

"Hi, Dad. I got some news. You wanna come in while I tell you both about it?"

Instead of answering, Grandpa spat again, got up, and followed him into the house.

"Hi, Mom," said Carroll, and kissed her on the cheek. She sat in her wheelchair, smiling happily.

"What's this news you got?" asked Grandpa.

Uncle Carroll handed Grandma a small package. "You're a blue-star mother now. I've joined the Army Air Corps."

She opened the package and took out an eight-inch square of cotton edged with a red fringe. A blue star on a white background filled the center.

"You hang that in the front window, Mom, so's the whole world knows you got a son in the service."

"I don't want no son in the service."

"Ma, where's your patriotism? We're at war, you know."

"War or no, you're the last of the Smiths. You git killed and the line dies out."

"That's my other surprise. I've asked Helen to marry me. She said yes."

"Well, I swear," said Grandma.

"You join up to get an education?" I asked.

"How'd you get so smart?" he asked. "Yes, that's part of it, but I want to fight for my country too."

"When are you gitten married?" asked Grandma.

"When do you go into the service?" asked Grandpa.

"What are you gonna learn to be?" I asked.

"Whoa now. Wait a minute." Uncle Carroll stiffened his body into attention and saluted. "Navigator-bombardier Smith, at your service. They said I was too tall to be a pilot. I report in two weeks. We're getting married Sunday, right after church. I guess I might as well tell you, since you all know how to count anyway: Helen's already pregnant."

Silence took over until Grandpa broke it. "That's all well and good, son, but what's the news?" Everyone laughed, and started talking again. Grandma started planning a combined wedding and send-off dinner. Grandpa started telling a story of his Spanish-American war days, and I wondered who the hell would take me hunting now.

****

I was on my bicycle a full block away when I saw the Army car drive up to the house. I raced back to the front yard and let my bike drop, wheels still spinning. Grandma was just opening the front screen door.

"Mrs. Smith?"

"Yes."

"I regret to inform you that your son, Carroll, was killed in the crash of his B-17 bomber on a training flight over Texas."

"Oh, my Lord."

"I'm sorry, Mrs. Smith. His body will be shipped back in a sealed coffin. There was a fire."

"Dear Jesus."

"What address would you like the coffin shipped to?"

"I don't know. The Stauffer Funeral Home, I guess. They buried my daughter."

"Very well, Mrs. Smith. I see that you have a blue mother's star in your window. I've brought you a new one, a gold star."

The soldier opened the screen door just enough to hand it to her. She took it casually, as if it were a newspaper.

"I'll be in touch with you again when the body arrives. We'll see to it that he has a fine funeral. I'm sorry, Mrs. Smith."

With that, he turned, went to his car, and left. Grandma made no effort to move her wheelchair. My own insides were churning like they were making butter. I didn't know if this was happening or not. I was afraid either way. I waited to see what Grandma did.

"Come on in here, Sammy. Come sit in my lap."

I did. She stroked my hair and pulled my head close to her bosom.

"You're all I have left now, Sammy. Promise me you'll never go to war."

"I promise, Grandma. Is Uncle Carroll really dead?"

"Yes, son. He's dead."

She still did not cry, so I did not cry either. She had never called me son before. I didn't know how to take it, so I did nothing.

"Oh, my God. Oh, my Lord," she said, over, and over, and over.

I stayed on her lap for a half an hour, not wanting to move, not wanting to talk. Finally, she set me free and went to her bedroom. I couldn't hear her words, but I knew she was praying both Christian and Cherokee prayers.

****

At the funeral, I was determined not to cry in front of all those people. It was a military funeral, and I held out until they fired their rifles. The shots brought back all of the hunting and fishing that Uncle Carroll had done with me, and I broke down. I laid my forearm against a mausoleum wall and rested my forehead against it. I began crying for my loss, and yelling at God for letting it happen. Grandpa came quickly to me.

"Don't cry, Sam. It can't be helped. We all have to die."

"But Grandpa, I've lost so much. My momma, my dog, my daddy, and now Uncle Carroll. I just can't take it anymore."

"You have to be strong, Sammy, stronger than all the things that have hurt you. If you're not, you'll be of no help to anyone. Look at your Grandma. She ain't cried yet. It ain't natural. You oughtta be thinking of her. Dry your tears now, and try to help your Grandma to cry."

I straightened up and looked. Grandma was erect and dry-eyed in her wheelchair. There was not a trace of expression on her face, not even when she was looking straight at me. A chill of new fear went through me. *My God,* I though, *I don't want to lose Grandma too.* I went to her.

"Grandma? Grandma, I love you."

She didn't respond. Instead, she wheeled her chair to the edge of the grave, picked up a handful of dirt, and dropped it into the opening. Then, she took the corsage from her dress and dropped it in too. Without a word, she turned and wheeled her way back to the funeral car. Grandpa helped her in, and then put her chair in the back of a friend's pickup.

"Come on, Sam. Let's go home."

I got in slowly, reluctantly. What would I do if Grandma left me alone too?

****

Grandma didn't get better or worse. Her house and furniture were old and battered, mostly by us kids, but she always kept it clean. She said that she wanted to be able to have company at any time and not feel ashamed. Now, she let the windows get dirty, the cobwebs hang. The torn linoleum floor was stippled with stains, toys, and trash. Even the first-of-the-month pot roast was different. The vegetables were all mushy, and didn't hold their natural flavors anymore. She quit baking pies and cookies. All we got for breakfast were peanut butter sandwiches, which we had to make ourselves. Even the homemade bread got hard and stale in between.

I took it worse than the others did. I was always special; now I was nobody. I didn't know what to do to bring her back. She'd just sit in her wheelchair, seldom moving, just staring straight ahead without seeing anything. Finally, I tried to make her cry, just like Grandpa said.

"Grandma, why don't you cry for Uncle Carroll?"

"Oh, Sammy, you wouldn't understand. Cherokees have to touch their dead. Not only that, but I don't even know if my son is really in that coffin, or some stranger is. Dear God, I just don't know."

Then she shut up, and wouldn't say another word. I prayed that night for the wisdom to help her.

The following week, on a stormy Sunday night, everyone but Grandma and me were asleep in bed. I had my radio on to a weak, faraway station, playing classical music. My ear was right next to the radio when a thunderclap sounded right over the house. The windows shook and the doors rattled.

I ran to the front door and looked out its window to make sure the house was still in place. Lightning showed sheets of rain falling, and lit up the living room. As I turned to go back to bed, I saw Grandma sitting there.

"Grandma! You scared me!"

"Hush, Sammy. Do you see him?"

"See who?"

"Your Uncle Carroll."

"I don't see him"

"I do. He's right next to you. Hello, son."

I looked again, and saw nothing. Another flash showed Grandma's face set in a strange smile.

"I understand, son," she said. "Can I touch you? Can you touch me? Oh, son. Oh, Carroll. I love you. Can't you stay a little longer? Goodbye, son. Thank you. Thank you, dear Jesus. Come here, Sammy."

I sat on the footrest of her wheelchair and lay my head in her lap. "What'd you see, Grandma?"

"I saw your Uncle Carroll."

A chill went down my spine as I accepted that she really had seen him.

"What'd he say?"

"Oh, Sam, it was so beautiful. I couldn't tell who it was at first. I thought it might be my own beloved mother. The light was blue and shimmery, like a living fog. Then, his face came clear, and the upper part of his body. Then he spoke to me:

'Don't worry, Mother. The important part of me is here.'

"Then I saw that he had no legs. I asked about touchin'. He just smiled and shook his head no. All of a sudden, Sammy, my worries and fears were gone. They were taken away, just like they're taken away at a Cherokee burial. I felt…feel more peaceful than I can ever remember feelin'. Sammy, go to bed now. I want to cry."

I went to the kitchen and stood beside the door where I couldn't be seen. I listened to her cry for a long time. I cried, myself, as I heard her give prayer after prayer of gratitude and thanks. She was still praying when I went to bed, and fell into a profound sleep.

August 9th, 1930

On August 9th, 1930, a scream funneled out of the upstairs window of an isolated farmhouse. Zina's mother Sarah, a wheelchair-confined cripple, waited downstairs, hoping to hear a newborn cry. The only sound she heard was her husband, Rupert, and Joe in the kitchen.

"Don't worry, Joe," said Rupert. "There's a jug of tomato wine in the ice pit. You want some?"

"Sure."

The ice pit was under the house, and lined with bales of hay. The dank smell of the bottom layer overpowered the onions, potatoes, and other edibles stored in bins formed by the bales. Rupert extracted a jug labeled "TOMATO." He blew out the lamp as he climbed to the outside of the two-story, weather-beaten house.

Inside, he sat the jug on the kitchen table, and went to the cupboard to fetch two tumblers. "This oughtta make you feel better."

"Thanks, Dad. Wonder what's taking so blasted long?"

"She's new. Lots of heifers have trouble with their firstborn."

"Wish I had your calm about it."

"Wait'll you have a couple. Then you will."

They heard another scream. Joe set his wine down and turned pale. "What's wrong?"

"Ain't nothing wrong, Joe. It's coming, that's all."

Rupert pushed the tumbler towards him. Joe picked it up and drank it down like water. Sarah disapproved immediately.

"Shame on you men! You especially, Joe. Your wife's in hard labor, and you're sitting here, guzzling it down."

"Well, what the hell can I do, Ma?"

"Somebody downstairs bring me some more towels and hot water!" hollered the doctor.

"Do what he says," said Sarah. "You know where the towels are."

Joe got up, took a teakettle from the stove, and ran upstairs with it. Sarah wheeled over to the linen closet and took out every towel.

"Where the hell's the towels?" growled the doctor.

Joe, without answering, ran downstairs, grabbed the towels from Sarah, and ran back up again. "How's she doing, Doc?"

"Just fine. The head is just starting to move. Should be over with soon."

"Anything else I can do?"

"Not now. Leave me be."

When Joe was halfway down the stairs, Zina screamed again. Joe froze momentarily and then rushed the rest of the way to the kitchen table. Rupert had already poured another glass. Joe drank half of it down.

"Slow down, son. No use in getting drunk."

Another scream interrupted Joe's reply. He finished off his glass and shoved it over for more. "Goddamn. Why's it have to hurt like that? You think she's putting on?"

"No, she ain't putting on!" said Sarah angrily. "The Bible says we shall be in travail in childbirth. You think about what you did to make her this way. Then you can hang your head in shame."

"A husband's got rights!" snapped Joe, also angry.

Rupert laughed. "You got the right to feed and clothe your family, that's all. I ain't touched Sarah in fifteen years."

"You ain't never gonna touch me again, either, Mr. Smith," said Sarah.

This time, Rupert drained his glass.

"Joe, come up here!" yelled the doctor. "Bring a lamp."

Joe complied. He was there for over ten minutes. When he returned, his face was ashen and he was trembling.

"What's wrong, Joe?" asked Sarah.

"The baby's not coming. It's stuck. She's too small for it. The doctor says it's because she's seventeen. My God, what am I gonna do?"

"Sit down and take it easy," said Rupert.

"You don't understand!" yelled Joe. "The doctor told me to decide which one I wanted to save, my wife or my baby."

"Dear Jesus," said Sarah. "What did you tell him?"

"I told him that if I can't have both, I don't want neither."

"You bastard!" yelled Sarah. "You've killed my girl! Take me upstairs, both of you."

Sarah lifted her body on to a chair.

Rupert moved first, and bumped up the stairs with the wheelchair. He returned, and clasped hands with Joe to make a seat for Sarah. They moved up the stairs until she was back in her wheelchair.

"Get away now. Leave me be. Go back to your boozing."

Rupert and Joe left reluctantly. There was no quarter in Sarah's voice or eyes.

"What's wrong, Doctor?" she asked.

"She's too young. There's not enough pelvis. The baby's head is through, but its shoulders won't come."

"What are you going to do?"

"Use forceps. It may kill the baby, perhaps Zina too, but it's the only chance I have to save both of them."

"If you have to, Doctor, forget the baby. Save my daughter."

"That choice isn't yours, Sarah. Her husband has already made it. Zina doesn't belong to you anymore; she belongs to Joe."

Sarah wheeled to the head of the bed and took her daughter's hand. Zina was wet with sweat and tears, and was groaning softly. She had stuffed a towel in her mouth.

"Do what you have to do, Doctor," said Sarah in a flat voice.

The *doctor inserted* the forceps and manipulated them until the baby's head and neck were firmly in their grasp. Then, he started to pull. Zina screamed, the sound muffled by the towel.

"Come on, come on, come on," pleaded the doctor as he placed his foot on the end of the bed for more leverage. Finally the child, bleeding from the forceps, came out. Zina fainted.

Sarah cried. The doctor cleared the air passages, but no breath was taken. Slap. Slap again. No sound.

"Joe!" he hollered.

Joe bound up the steps, Rupert close behind.

"Get me some ice and fresh water. Rupert, empty out this basin."

"What is it, Doc?" asked Joe.

"It's dead," said the doctor. "Do what I say. It's my only chance to save him."

Joe started to speak again. Sarah interrupted him. "Run! Damn you! Run!"

Joe rushed to the ice pit, and retrieved a 20-pound chunk. He dumped it into a copper washtub. "Ice pick," he demanded. "Where the hell's the goddamned ice pick?"

"Take it easy. You'll get more done, and better too."

"YOU take it easy!" exploded Joe. "That's MY baby up there!"

Joe found the ice pick and savagely drove it into the chunk. "Don't ruin the washtub," cautioned Rupert. "I'm going up with the water. Come on."

The doctor laid the baby on the bed and poured steaming water into one basin and ice into the other. When they were full enough, he dunked the baby into the ice water, then into the near-scalding water. The baby gasped for breath, and then began crying.

The doctor, tears streaming down his face, wrapped it in a towel, handed it to Sarah, and attended to Zina. "You have a son, Joe."

Joe reached for the baby. Sarah held it away from him. "You gave him up, Joe. My daughter too. I ain't never gonna let you forget that."

Joe looked to Rupert for an ally. Rupert just turned his palms up and shrugged.

"Ma," said Zina, "is the baby alright?"

"Just fine, honey. You can take him now." Sarah looked again at Joe, her face a frozen commitment. "Never."

Christmas, 1939

Billy and Dan were best friends. Indeed, Dan was the only friend Billy had. Dan's father worked for the WPA, the Works Project Administration, fathered by President Roosevelt to boost the USA out of the Great Depression. Billy's dad didn't work at all. He was an alcoholic jailbird. Billy was glad to see him go to jail. The beatings stopped then.

Dan looked forward to Christmas. His wish list included a bike, a BB gun, and a pocketknife. He knew he would get one of them. He dreamed he would get all three. Billy expected nothing. Religion, especially Christianity, was not tolerated in his tar-paper shack of a home. Neither was 'Toys for Needy Children'. Billy's dad said, "If'n I cain't give 'im nothing', then nobody's gonna give 'im nothing,"

Dan knew this. He told Billy, "If'n I git 'em, you can ride my bike and shoot my BB gun and whittle with my knife."

Christmas grew near and Dan's dad got laid off. Dan's mother got sick at the same time. His dad gave him the bad news: "Son, don't expect much for Christmas. Your mom's gonna be in the hospital and I just ain't got no money." Billy gave Dan some good news. His dad had been arrested in a drunken brawl in a barroom. He would be gone for ninety days. Dan told him of his own father's job loss and no Christmas presents forthcoming. He was almost crying.

"Don't cry, Dan. We got each other, you know." Billy put his arm around Dan's shoulder. And Dan didn't cry.

Dan had a special relationship with his grandmother. She was old, poor, half-Indian, and lived her life in a wheelchair.

Christmas, 1939

"Be there a reason why you boys can't make something for each other?" she asked when Dan came to her in despair.

The lights came on for Dan. He could hardly wait to tell Billy. Billy's lights came on, too. "Let's keep it a secret," he said. "Let's really surprise each other."

Christmas came. Dan got fruits and hard candy, socks and underwear. Billy got nothing. That afternoon, Billy and Dan met under the scoreboard in the snow-covered baseball field. Each had a small package. Dan's was wrapped in the Sunday comics section, Billy's was in a brown paper bag.

"Hi, Dan! Merry Christmas!"

"Hi, Billy! Merry Christmas to you, too."

Both held onto their gifts, not quite knowing how to present them. Billy finally held his out and said, "Here."

"Thanks, Billy. Here's yours."

Dan opened his first. It was a rubber band shooter made out of wood. It shot bands cut out from inner tubes. "Just what I always wanted!" he said. "How did you know? Open yours, quick."

Billy tore the paper off, opened the box inside, and yelled, "Thank you! Thank you!" In the box was a forked branch trimmed into a Y-shaped slingshot. "I love you, Dan!"

"I love you, too, Billy. Think we could go down to Stink Crick and shoot some frogs?"

"We gotta ask our folks, first."

"OK. Hurry up. I'll meet you there."

It started snowing again while they were at the creek. Huge flakes came down from a windless sky and coated them with purity. The water ran a sluggish black between white-coated banks. There were no frogs, of course, but they didn't care. They had each other.

Eternal Water

There was a drop of water, once, that knew it was alive. It lived in a great ocean and carried in itself the salt of the earth and the treasures of the sea. It was quite happy to be alive.

One day, the sun came out and was hotter than usual. The drop evaporated. It was changed into vapor and sucked up into the sky. It was very afraid, because it had to leave behind everything it knew that was good and beautiful.

Up, up into the sky it flew where it became colder and colder and was turned into part of a cloud. The winds blew it about helter-skelter. Soon, it forgot where it came from and surrendered to its fate.

It seemed like forever until it was changed into a drop of rain. It fell into the dirtiest part of a dirty city. Instead of salt and treasure, it now carried germs and disease and became extremely unhappy.

"Why is this happening to me?" it cried out. "I know I was not meant for this. I don't know how I know, but I know I know it."

Winter came and the drop of water was frozen into ice. It lost all of its knowledge and lay in silence for what seemed forever.

Then the sun came again. The ice melted. The little drop was evaporated once again and left behind all of its dirtiness, for which it was very glad. It became a cloud again and was blown half-way around the world.

"I want to be beautiful again." it prayed. "How can I become beautiful?"

A raindrop next to it heard and answered, "You must become

a snowflake. It will only last for a short time, but you will be beautiful."

One day the cloud blew over Minnesota and the drop of water was changed into a snowflake. "Am I beautiful now?" it asked another snowflake. "I cannot see myself."

"I see that you are very beautiful," said the other. "I cannot see myself either. Am I beautiful, too?"

"Oh, yes! And so are all the other snowflakes I see. And I see that they are all different, even though they are all the same. How wonderful!"

Then the snow fell on Minnesota, with all the beautiful flakes coming down together to dress the land in white. Beneath the snowfall, a young boy played and stuck out his tongue. The flake fell on it, gave up its coldness and changed back into a drop of water.

"My beauty is gone," it cried. "Everything is ruined. I wish I had never left the sea."

"Foolish, little drop of water," said another snowflake on the boy's tongue, just before it melted. "It is better to be useful than beautiful. You do not know how truly fortunate you are. You could have fallen onto a glacier and been locked up forever. Instead, you have been given life to travel over and over until you have been everything you can be and gone everywhere you can go. You know the sun, the wind, the cold. You have been rich and poor. You will be rich and poor again. You must learn to enjoy everything you become. You are alive and that is all that really matters."

Then the boy closed his mouth and swallowed, and the little drop of water was off on a brand-new adventure, in a secret place that it had never been to before.

Fighting for Fun

Me and a few other boys, sittin' on the steps of the Southside Baptist Church, held a spittin' contest. The sidewalk in front of us showed dozens of dark spots where the spit hadn't dried yet under the hot July sun of St. Joseph, Missouri.

"My granpa chews tobacco," I said. "You should see him spit. We got wasps that live in the ground in our front yard. Granpa sits on the porch and spits tobacco juice on 'em when they come out of the ground."

"Ain't he afraid of getting stung?"

"'Course not. Me and my two sisters ain't afraid neither. We sit real still and the wasps come and light on our skin. We ain't never been stung yet. Granpa taught us that. He ain't afraid of nothin'."

"Boy, you wouldn't catch me doin' that! I hate wasps and bugs and spiders."

"You couldn't live at my house then. We got all three of 'em and all kinds at that," I said. "'Specially in the cellar. I don't like goin' down there."

"Hey! Look at how far I can spit!" said Norm. He threw his head forward as he spit and landed further than anyone else had.

"You cheated!" I yelled. "You moved your head. Besides, you're standin' on the wrong step. You're closer than anyone else."

"Don't you call me a cheat," warned Norm.

"I wouldn't call you one if you wasn't one."

"Oh, yeah?"

"Yeah."

"Wanna make somethin' of it?"

"You wanna fight?" I asked.

"I can whip you any old time."

"I beat up on Mike. I'm ten and he's thirteen and I whipped him good."

"Betcha can't do it to me."

"Betcha I can. You have to hit me first, though. Daddy said I can't never start a fight, but I can't ever run away from one neither."

"Where do you want me to hit you?" asked Norm.

"On my shoulder."

Both of us moved out to the green grass between the sidewalk and street. The other boys gathered around us in a circle, egging us on.

"Well," I said, "you gonna hit me or not?"

The preacher came out to get into his car parked across the street. "What's going on here?" he demanded. "You boys would be better off inside the church instead of on the steps in front of it. You quit that spitting, you hear?"

"Yes, sir," came the chorus.

We broke formation and waited until he drove away.

"You still wanna fight?" asked Norm.

"I don't care," I said.

"Me neither," said Norm.

"Well, I do," said Clay, the biggest and heaviest kid of the lot. "Who wants to fight me?"

"Not me," came another chorus.

"What about you, Sam?" asked Clay.

"Yeah, Sam. Go ahead," said the group.

"We ain't got nothin' to fight about," I said.

"Oh, yeah? Where'd you git those rabbit teeth and big ears? Your mama a jackass? Your daddy a rabbit?"

I felt myself flush. "Don't you talk about my mother. She's dead."

"Jackass, jackass, son of a mule."

"Shut up!"

I rushed him. Clay sidestepped and hit me in the side of the head, throwing me off balance. I recovered quickly and used the same windmill technique I'd used on Mike. It worked, but not before I got a black eye and Clay a bloody nose. We quit fighting at the same time, neither of us a clear-cut winner.

"Boy! You sure do know how to hit!" said Clay, holding his nose.

"You, too," I said, holding my eye.

"Shake and make up?" asked Clay, holding out his hand.

"Sure," I said and took the offered palm.

****

"I got into a fight today," I told my dad that night as he looked sharply at my face.

"Yeah, I see you did. What did I tell you about fighting?"

"Not to."

"Who started it?"

"He did."

"You whup him?"

"No, sir. We came out even, but he's bigger than me."

"What was it about?"

I was leery about the name calling. "Spittin'," I said. I told him most of the rest of the story and he laughed when I was done.

"Well, I ain't sayin' as how I approve, but I'm sure glad you ain't no chicken. You gonna have to fight him again?"

"Nope. We're best friends now."

"Well, if that don't beat all!"

"How come?" I asked.

"Here I teach you not to fight and you go ahead and fight anyway, and make the guy that gives you a black eye your best friend. That ain't what fightin's supposed to be about."

"Maybe fightin's different for kids than it is for grownups."

He looked surprised. "Yeah, son. Maybe it is...maybe it is."

Grandma, 1935

"Grandma, can I ask you a question?"

"What, Jackie?"

"Grandma, how come you have to use crutches?"

Her dark eyes tightened, and then closed. "Well," she said, "if you're old enough to ask, you're old enough to know. God punished me for something, and to this day, I don't know what for. It came to pass that I needed an operation. Something was wrong inside my belly. Well, they gave me a shot in the spine, low down. The needle slipped, or the doctor didn't know what he was doing, or God guided his hand. Anyway, the shot paralyzed me from the waist down. I was bedfast with two wonderful children to care for.

"I was bedfast for a long time…years. Grandpa was good to me back then. He was good to the kids too, your mother and Uncle Carroll. Then one day, he started to get mean to me. He'd come into my bedroom where I lay helpless and start yelling at me. He said horrible things about my not being a real wife, mother, or even a woman. And he wouldn't stop. Finally, it was every single day, morning and night. I just couldn't take it anymore.

"One day, I hauled myself out of my bed with just my arms while he and the kids were away. Then I crawled to the kitchen, my whole lower body just dragging behind. I was gonna fix his supper, but I couldn't. I couldn't reach anything. So I just laid there and cried.

"He came home and found me there. I thought he was gonna yell at me some more, but he didn't. He just stood there, looking at me, not saying a word. I was ashamed to look up at him. The mess I'd made on my clothes only proved his point. I wasn't a woman anymore.

Grandma, 1935

"He stood there, quiet, for so long that I finally had to look up at him. He was crying without making a sound. I never saw him cry before or since. He was still crying when he helped me back to bed.

"I didn't understand it at first. It took the longest time for it to sink in that he was right. I wasn't a woman anymore. I wasn't a real woman. I was only a bedfast cripple. Right then and there I decided that I wasn't gonna lay in bed until I died.

"To this day, he won't tell me how he got the money to do it, but he hired a doctor to come out to the farmhouse. Hour after hour, day after day, the doctor pushed and pulled and twisted and shoved my back and legs. Pain like you wouldn't believe.

"Do you know about pain, Jackie? I don't think so. You know what hurt is when you stub your toe or get spanked, but real pain is different. Real pain doesn't just happen to your body, it happens to your mind too. I pray to God you never have to go through it.

"Anyway, Grandpa stopped yelling at me. The kids started telling me I would walk again. I started half believing it. Oh, Jesus, forgive my unbelief!

"Finally, I was able to use crutches and a wheelchair. The more I did it, the easier it got. I needed help in bathing and Grandpa was glad to do that. He kept wanting to touch me on my privates. I wouldn't allow that. I thought that maybe that was what God was punishing me for.

"Then one day, I had a vision. I saw my own dear mother, a full-blooded Cherokee and daughter of a chief. I was wide-awake when it happened. She didn't say anything to me. She just kind of floated there in mid-air, but I sensed what she was trying to tell me. She was saying to turn my back on the white man's ways and go back to the Indian ways. So I did. Then, with the Depression and all, Grandpa had no job. With no money coming in, we picked poke greens and paw-paws and mushrooms and berries and black walnuts and wild honey. I rendered my own lard from hogs Grandpa got for working on farms. I made my own soap using our woodstove ashes. And lots and lots of stuff more. When you're a little bigger, you'll learn to do all those things and hunt too. I'll bet you'll be a great hunter."

Just then, a knock on the screen door made it rattle.

"It's me, Miz Smith. Julie. Miz Smith, Sadie's in some real fierce pain. She wants you to come right away so's you can pray for her."

"Oh, dear Jesus. Jackie, get your shirt on. You have to come with me."

I caught the tone of her voice and moved fast to obey. She rolled her chair over to the corner where her crutches were and heaved her big body up on them.

"Hurry up, Jackie."

I held the screen door open for her and watched her slug her way down the three porch steps. She walked by throwing one leg ahead at a time, then moving her crutches one at a time. It was a slow pace, giving me plenty of time to look around.

Grandma's house always looked out of place. It looked ugly when you compared it to the houses around it. They were all clean and mostly white. They had picket fences covered in whitewash and green lawns that were always mowed. We had nothing but hard-packed dirt where a few dandelions grew.

Between the curb and sidewalk, there were lots of trees. They were oak and elm and cottonwood and some more I didn't know the names of. They made the sidewalk a lot cooler. When we left our own neighborhood, in about five blocks, the poor peoples' houses started. They always made me glad I didn't live there. There were no more trees or lawns or fences, just hedges that were never trimmed. Their front lawns were hard ground, just like ours. Sadie's home looked the worst of the lot.

We heard Sadie screaming two houses away. It seemed she didn't hardly stop to take a breath. Grandma started to walk a little faster but I lagged behind. I was afraid of all that pain. When we reached the porch, Grandma put both crutches under one arm and waited for me to catch up. By now, I could hear the words inside the screams.

"Jesus, dear God, take me! Oh, please, please let me die!"

Grandma, 1935

"You stay here, Jackie. Wait on the porch. Sadie, I'm here. I'm here, Sadie." I listened to Grandma starting to pray. "Oh, please, dear Jesus, have mercy on this poor soul. End her suffering and take her into your loving arms."

The prayers did no good. The screams continued. I looked through the screen. There was an awful stench, like rotting garbage, only worse. I saw Sadie lying on her back. I watched her scream and beat the air with her fists. I watched Grandma sitting on a chair at the edge of the bed, hands first together in prayer, then touching her friend like she was trying to make the pain go away. Grandma prayed as much as Sadie screamed. She finally stopped praying.

"Sadie, I have to go now. The girls will be coming home soon and it ain't right for Jackie to be hearing all of this. Try to get some rest, dear."

"Oh, God! Don't leave me Sarah!"

"I have to, dear. Zina's bringing the girls over."

Sadie's little release from the pain finally ceased. She began screaming again and her prayers changed. "Oh, Satan! Please help me, Satan! Take me to your bosom and let me die. God doesn't care. Take me, Satan!"

Grandma leaned forward from her chair beside the bed and slapped Sadie hard in the face. "Shut up!" she yelled. "Oh, God, I pray for your forgiveness from this blasphemy. Forgive her for she knows not what she says."

"Forgive me, Lord," prayed Sadie. "Forgive me and end my torment. Take me, please, take me."

Grandma, crying, heaved to her crutches and left, promising to come back as soon as possible. She joined me on the front porch. I kept quiet on the way back home, wondering what to say.

"Grandma, what's wrong with Aunt Sadie?"

"She's got cancer, honey, real bad. It's so bad the pain killers don't work anymore. Poor soul. Her whole belly's being eaten up inside."

"Why doesn't God help her?"

"I don't know, Jackie. I just don't know."

I was quiet for a little bit, then I said, "I hate God."

"Jackie, don't talk like that! It's a sin."

"I don't care. God lets too many bad things happen. I hate God."

I began to cry. Grandma looked at me quick-like, and then she started to cry too. We walked side-by-side all the way back to our own neighborhood before we stopped crying.

Jack Dukes

The Backward Elephant

The herd of female elephants gathered in a clump of trees for shelter from the hot African sun. One of them, Lulumulu, was about to give birth. It was to be her first birth, and she was a little afraid. Zamboa, the oldest elephant, and leader of the herd, told her not to worry.

"I've had a dozen births already, and nothing has gone wrong."

Still, Lulumulu was afraid something was wrong…and she was right. For hours, she labored in the heat, but the baby elephant would not come out. She grew thirsty. Three of the elephants left for the waterhole, where they filled their trunks, and then carried it back and squirted it into the mouth of Lulumulu, who was quite grateful for it.

The sun went down, and she was still in labor. Finally, the pain got so bad that she began to moan in the low, rumbling voice that only elephants can hear. It was more than Zomboa could stand.

"Listen to me, all you lady elephants. Here's what I want you to do. Split up on both sides of Lulumulu, put your trunks against her belly, and push hard. Maybe we can help her out that way."

The elephants were quite amazed, for no one had ever done that before. They all thought that Zamboa was the wisest old elephant in the world. They did as she suggested, and an hour later, Rapakak was born, tail end first. He was perfect, and healthy, although he was not to believe it himself. When he went to nurse from his mother, he backed up into her breast.

"What are you doing, child?" she exclaimed.

"I'm going to nurse, mother."

"Well, you can't do it that way. Turn around."

"But, mother…"

"Turn around!"

After he had finished nursing, he backed away from his mother, looked up at her and said "You're mean, you know. You should be ashamed for making a poor baby nurse with his hind end."

"What on earth are you talking about?"

"Babies get born head first. My tail came out first, so that's my head. Now, I have to go through life eating with my tail end, drinking with my tail end, and talking through my tail end. I'm the unhappiest little elephant in the world."

His mother tried to talk him out of it, her friends tried to talk him out of it, and even his father came by, and after he stopped laughing, he tried to talk Rapakak out of it, but nothing worked.

Old Zamboa, wise with the experience of her years, dreamed up a plan. She sent Rapaka out to a melon field, one of his favorite foods, and she told him she was going to use magic to cure him when he got back. While he was gone, she told the rest of the herd her plan. They were all ready for him when he returned.

They formed a circle around him. Zamboa stepped into the circle too.

"Rapakak, here's what I'm going to do. I'm going to stick my trunk down your throat so far that I can grab your tail. Then, I'm going to give it a big jerk and turn you inside out. When I am done, your front end will be your head, and your back end will be your tail. Do you understand?"

"Will it hurt?"

"Of course it will hurt, but not too much. You will feel a pressure in your throat, your tail will be jerked, and your hind end will feel like its being slapped. Ready?"

"I guess so."

Zamboa didn't hesitate. She shoved her trunk deep into his throat. At the same time, one of the other elephants grabbed his tail and jerked it really hard. Two more elephants slapped him on the rump so hard that he staggered a little. Just then, Zamboa jerked her trunk out.

"There!" she said. "It's all over. Do you feel better now?"

Rapakak, who has closed his eyes when he felt he tail being jerked, opened them and looked around.

"You mean I'm cured?" he said.

"Sure as watermelons," said his mother.

"Thank you, Zamboa."

"You're welcome," she said. "Now go play."

From that day on, Rapakak had his head on straight, and no one ever heard of him complain about it again.

Easter Blossom

The racing brown waters swirled by the bow of my runabout as I stepped onto a steep, sloping bank with anchor in hand. The earth crumbled beneath my feet. I dropped in an instant up to my hips in the flooding Mississippi River. Quickly, I tossed the anchor with my right hand as my left clutched and dug for traction, finally stopping my fall with one small tuft of grass. My right hand began searching for something more to hang on to, and found nothing.

I needed only a few more inches to reach the line of bushes the anchor had grabbed into, but the merciless water dragged me sideways even as gravity pulled me towards the bottom of the sixty-foot depths.

So much for an Easter Sunday boatride, I thought, as another part of my mind raced for a way out. No one knows where I am. I have no ID on me. I'll just be another unidentified corpse found at Lock and Dam number three.

The gravel and sand beneath me was eroding away faster now, as my body forced the current into the bank. If I let go, my chest waders would fill with water and leave me without hope. I vaguely wondered why I didn't feel panic.

Afraid to switch hands, I passed my right hand over my left to see if anything grew there that I could hang on to. The way my head was pressed against the ground left me no chance to turn my head and see. The back of my hand scraped under something that stung like little electric shocks. A thistle, I guessed, and it was: a deep-rooted plant with a stem strong enough to hold me – if I could only hold on to it.

Carefully, I wrapped the palm and fingers of my hand around it. It was like holding stinging bees. Before I could change my mind, I let go with my left hand. As soon as my fill weight was on my right hand, I used the leverage to lunge upwards. My right hand was on fire. My left flailed around and found a bush no larger than my thumb. I had to let go of the thistle.

"Please hold," I prayed, as my full weight came upon the shrub. I felt some of its roots let go, and then hold again. My right hand found another bush. Inch by inch, I pulled myself up the bank until my knees reached relatively solid ground, and the danger had passed.

I picked the flower I was after, retrieved the runabout, and headed back to my houseboat. I put the flower in a bud vase and waited for Sara Jane to return from church.

"Oh, what a pretty flower!" she said. "Where did you find it in all of this flood?"

"On a high bank in the river," I said. "I didn't even have to get my feet wet. Happy Easter!

Blackie

It was the end of a long, hard Saturday. Doc, Blackie, and me were in the office part of the pet hospital. Doc had his gin bottle out. Every once in a while, he'd take a swig from it.

"Here, Shadow, have a little nip."

I was surprised when he did that. Colored people had separate fountains, toilets, and schools and hat to sit in the balcony at the movies, and at the back in the bus. Now, Doc was offering him a drink from the same bottle.

"No, thank you, boss. Old Blackie, he don't drink very much."

Shadow was Doc's pet name for Blackie, because he was so silent when he went about his work of cleaning the cages and feeding the animals. Doc hired him so I'd have more time to help out with treatments, operations, and farm calls.

"I'd like a swig," I said.

He almost gave me the bottle, and then jerked it back. "You're too young to drink. How old are you, Shadow?"

"Ah, don't rightly know, Doc. Mah mammy and pappy, they was slaves. Ah got taken away when I was a baby. Ah figures close to a hundred."

"Too bad you're not a horse. I could tell your age from your teeth."

Doc laughed at his own joke. Blackie smiled a huge grin. His teeth were large and yellow. He wasn't very big, which made his teeth seem even bigger. He was skinny, and very black. His hair was snow white, and lay in tight curls against his scalp.

"Naw, Doc. I ain't no horse."

Blackie

"I know you're not, Shadow. You know what you are? You're a perfect slave. I couldn't find a better man than you for the work you do. You sleep on a cot in the back room, you eat the same horsemeat that we feed to the dogs, you almost never get sick, you don't gamble or drink, you never ask for a raise, and I don't have to pay into Social Security for you."

"Yas, suh, that's old Blackie all right."

Doc finished off the last of the gin. "Well, Shadow, the boy and I are going home. You take good care of the place now."

"Yas suh, Doc. Goodnight."

****

Blackie was there alone when I got back from high school the following Monday.

"Hi, Blackie!"

"Good afternoon, Mistuh Sam!"

"The dogs OK?"

"Yas suh. 'Cept for that big grey one. He's jus' plumb mean."

"You clean his cage?"

"Naw suh. I's too skeered."

"OK. I'll do it. Want to help?"

"Not rightly, Mistuh Sam, but ah reckon ah will anyway."

"Good for you, Blackie. Fetch me the choke pole."

The choke pole was six feet long. It has a rope secured to the end. About a foot from the end, a hole was bored through the pole. The rope passed through the hole so that a noose was formed. To use it, the noose was passed over the dog's head and pulled tight. It tied the end of the pole to the animal's neck so that it could neither run, nor charge.

While Blackie fetched the pole, I fixed up a shot of penicillin. The dog was a boxer: young, muscular, vicious, and in no mood to be treated. I lay the syringe on the next cage and took the pole from Blackie. I slipped it between the bars, noosed the boxer, and handed the pole to Blackie.

"Hold on tight now. I don't want to get bit."

"Yas suh, Mistuh Sam. Ah hold on good."

I opened the door just far enough to scrape out the newspapers and dung, and then laid down fresh paper. The boxer was snarling and jumping, making Blackie hold on for dear life. Then, I picked up the syringe.

"Hold his head in the far corner so's his ass is at me," I said.

With the dog in position, I injected him in the rump muscle. I closed the cage, took the pole, and released the noose. The dog bit at its rear end from the sting of the medicine.

"That's good, Mistuh Sam. You sure know how to handle them."

"Thanks, Blackie." I noticed something different about him. "What's that lump on your cheek?"

"Ah gots a bad tooth, Mistuh Sam. Doc, he's gonna pull it for me."

"I knew he pulls dog teeth. I never knew he pulled human teeth."

"Oh, Doc, he do everything for me. Old Blackie git sick, Doc, he fix it up just fine."

"There's Doc now. Hi, Doc! Blackie here, he needs a tooth pulled."

"All right, all right. Just give me chance to get settled down."

Doc went for his gin bottle, and took a hefty swig. "You're gonna have to come along on these farm calls, Sam. I'm going too old and fat to do it by myself anymore."

"Sure, Doc. Just get me out of school, that's all. Can I watch you pull Blackie's tooth?"

"You want to hold his head so that he doesn't bite me?"

I was startled for an instant, and then relaxed when I saw Blackie grinning. "I ain't gonna bite," he said.

"Open your mouth," said Doc.

Doc started wiggling the teeth one by one with his fingers. When he got to the bad one, Blackie moaned.

"OK," said the Doc. "It's pretty loose. Son, fetch me the tooth puller. You want procaine?" he asked Blackie.

"Naw suh. Ah don't need nothin'."

"You ever brush your teeth?" Doc asked Blackie.

"Naw suh. Ah ain't never learned how."

"Me neither," I grinned.

Doc looked at me sharply, and then turned back to Blackie.

"Open wide."

Doc slipped the jaws around the bad tooth, worked it hard back and forth, and then yanked it out in one hard pull. Blackie moaned the whole time, but didn't move his head. Doc handed him the gin bottle.

"Go rinse your mouth out with this. Swallow a little too. It'll make the pain seem less. I'll fix some saline solution for regular rinsing."

Blackie said nothing, but took the bottle and went into the back room.

"How long has it been since you've seen a dentist?" he asked me.

"I went once when I was in grade school."

"I've got a dentist friend I want you to go to. Will you do it?"

"Sure, I guess so. Why not?"

"Well, you'd better. Unless you want a mouthful of snags and empty spots, like Blackie has."

"I'd better go see how he's doing."

"Yes, you do that, son."

****

"How you doing, Blackie?"

"Oh, I's just fine, Mistuh Sam."

"You know, it's funny how you and me's so much alike."

"How's zat, suh?"

"Well, we're both orphans, to start with. My mommy died when I was nine, and my daddy run off and deserted us. For another thing, we both got bad breath. Billie told me so."

"Well, suh, we gits 'long just fine, don't we?"

"We sure do. Tell you what, Blackie, do you think I could eat some of that horsemeat sometime? I ain't never had none."

"Sho thing, Mistuh Sam. I'll save some out of the next batch for you. Cook it a little better than we do for the dogs."

"Thanks."

****

Three Saturdays later, I came in for my afternoon shift, the dental work all done.

"Hi, Doc!"

"Hello, son. How are the teeth coming?"

"He's all done. I needed fourteen fillings. I asked him if he could do anything with my buck teeth, but he said no."

"He teach you about brushing?"

"Sure did. Gramma and Granpa both has false teeth, so they don't know nothing about brushing. I brush morning and night now. I taught my sisters how to brush too. They mostly only do it when I holler at them though. At night, mostly. Where's Blackie?"

"Blackie's dead."

"No," I said. "That can't be true. I like Blackie a whole lot."

"It's true," said Doc. "I found him on his cot this morning when I opened up. He died in his sleep last night."

"Shit!" I said, and blinked back tears. I picked up the bottle of alcohol from the table and threw it against the opposite wall. "God damn death. I hate it." It shattered on the word damn.

"We all have to go sometime, son. You've seen death a lot in this hospital. Blackie is no different."

"What'd you do with him?"

"The county came and got him. They'll put him in a pauper's grave."

"Ain't there gonna be no funeral?"

"No. There's no one to care."

"I care."

"I know you do, son. I care too. But we can't afford a funeral for him just to show we cared."

"It ain't fair."

"Toughen up, son. Toughen up."

Courage

My study habits finally became solid enough for me to frequent the draw poker establishments that studded the streets of Monterey, California. My inept play slowly transformed into the kind of professional style that I had to develop if winning was the true goal. For me, it was. I had to win.

One Saturday night, at about 11:30, the game was interrupted by a visit form a drunken barracks mate. I went in with three aces and there was about $200 in the pot. The player ahead of me drew two cards. Three other players threw in, and the man behind me drew one card. That's when my friend appeared.

"Hi, Sam! How you doin'?" His speech was slurred and his balance unsteady.

"What the hell do you want, Charlie?"

"You go ahead and play. I can wait."

My concentration had been broken. I failed to observe my opponents as they squeezed out their new cards. The opener, the two-card draw, bet fifty. I wanted to raise, but decided against it. I called. The one-card draw raised one hundred. Two-cards called. If I called and lost, my winnings for the night were gone.

"Damn you, Charlie, you just blew my game all to hell."

I called. The first man held three fours and the other held three tens. He'd kept a kicker, just like I did. As soon as I started raking in the pot, Charlie came around the table, knelt, and put his arm around my shoulder.

"That's a boy, Sam! You know how to play 'em. Good old Sam. Sam, you gotta take me home."

"I don't gotta do nothing." He paid no attention.

"Sam, I got some Japs mad at me. I cussed them out for Pearl Harbor and Bataan and for being yellow cowards, and some other shit too. They're laying for me, Sam. They told me so."

"Well, shit. What the fuck's the matter with you? Niseis are just as American as you and me. You're crazy drunk, that's what's the matter. Shit."

"Take me home, Sam. Don't let them get me."

"Well, how in hell am I gonna do that? How many are there?"

"Bout twelve, I guess. Maybe fifteen."

"Yeah, and most of 'em know judo. For Christ's sake."

"You gonna play or fold?" asked the dealer.

"Cash me in. I got a batch of trouble that just landed on my head."

He cashed me in with good grace, and the players bid me good night. They knew I'd be back, and maybe my luck wouldn't be running so good next time. Charlie stumbled as he started to stand up. I just barely managed to support him. Finally, I got one of his arms around my shoulder and held it fast by his wrist. My other arm went around his waist.

"Can you walk, Charlie? C'mon. You can do better than that."

His full weight was falling on me with every other step. We managed to negotiate the tables and get out onto the street. The Monterey fog was heavy and the fish stink strong from the cannery. But the coolness seemed to help him clear his head. He began walking with me instead of dragging me down. Then, he started singing. Not soft lullabies, but raucous, dirty drinking songs. A few feet away, the fog soaked up the notes, but to my ears, they were advertisements of where we were.

"Shut up, Charlie. I've got to think." He quieted down briefly, while my mind spun through the likelihoods.

There was only one entrance to Presidio: up a blacktopped hill, and then a flight of about twelve steps. There were bushes on each side, tall and thick enough to hide an ambush. As we reached the beginning of the hill, Charlie started singing again. I stopped us dead in our tracks and clipped him one right on the jaw. It did no good whatsoever.

"What'd you do that for?" he asked in a subdued voice.

"Shut up, Charlie. If they're there, they know for certain we're coming now."

"Shit, I don't care. I got my buddy Sam looking out for me." He began singing again.

We got all the way up the hill without getting stopped. Maybe they're not there. I hoped against hope. Then I saw them: a bunch of dim figures at the top of the stairs, quiet and unmoving in the dense fog. I stopped at the bottom of the steps.

"Who's there?" one demanded.

"Sam Senior. I'm bringing home a drunken buddy."

"What's his name?"

I thought of lying, but kicked the thought out right away. They could find out the lie too easily, and might then make me a target.

"Charlie."

"We want him."

"You can't have him."

"How are you going to stop us?"

"Maybe I can't, but you'll have to go through me to get to him."

"We can do that."

"You have no reason to. He'll be around tomorrow, and sober then too. What's the sense in roughing up someone too drunk to even know it?"

I heard a flurry of whispers. The same voice spoke again. "Just give him to us. We'll take him to the barracks."

I was tempted, but only briefly. Charlie had shut up just ahead of the first accost, and had now slumped down into a dead weight, silent and practically asleep. My arms ached. If I let them have him and he got hurt, well, I just couldn't live with that.

"Sorry. I said I'd take him home, and that's just what I'm going to do."

"We're going to take him."

Courage

"Listen, he told me what went on. I got no appetite for what he said, but he's my buddy and I gotta care for him. You go ahead and do what you gotta do, but I'm coming up."

Charlie stumbled on the first step, and almost threw me off balance. The group at the top spread out along the top step so that I'd have to go through then. I was thankful they hadn't rushed us.

I practically dragged Charlie up the first three steps. Then, he woke up a little and started to help lift his own weight. I shot a short, silent prayer: please, God, don't let him start singing again.

At the next step, I had to stop. Two men stood shoulder to shoulder in front of me.

"Well," I said. "I guess this is it. You fellows either do what you have to do or get the hell out of my way. I'm coming through."

I put my foot on the top step, practically stepping on the shoe of one of the men. Just as my chest touched him, he stepped back to the side. His buddy did the same. Thank you God, I though passionately. The rest of the way to the barracks was without incident.

Charlie's bunk was on the first floor, mine on the second. I dropped him on his bunk, lifted his feet onto it, and stood there for a second, breathing hard and trembling all over. Charlie was out of it, passed out cold. I took a deep breath and headed upstairs to my bunk.

I'd no sooner undressed and lay down than I heard a commotion downstairs. I went down naked. The Nisei boys had Charlie in the brightly lit shower room. He and four of them were naked. They were all under the shower, which I sensed was a cold one. They were scrubbing him down with a GI floor brush. Yamashita said something in Japanese to the others and they all turned to stare. Finally, Yamashita grinned.

"You're some kind of brave bastard," he said. "We respect that."

I grinned back, turned around, and went back to my bunk.

"Brave," I thought. "We respect that."

I fell asleep, feeling oh-so-good.

Party

At first, in grade school, I didn't know that being poor meant being different. I laughed and played and fought with my boy friends, and we got along just swell. But the older I got, the more I sensed the difference. Pretty soon, I realized that the only friends I had were other poor boys. I suppose the other guys weren't rich, but they were rich to me. Gramma always said they were. Sometimes, I looked at them and felt ashamed of my own clothes and of always wanting the stuff that they had: bicycles and vacations, and a mommy and a daddy. Gramma and granpa tried hard, but it just wasn't the same.

Billy was my best friend. He knew a lot of stuff I didn't know. He never tried to be friendly with the rich kids like I did. They were polite to me, but that's all. I never got invited to their houses or picked to play in their games. Billy didn't either, but he didn't care. I guess he thought that he was better than them, no matter how much money they had. Then came the day when I got an invitation. I couldn't believe it at first, but when I did, I couldn't wait to tell Billy.

"I've been invited to Ramona's birthday party!"

"You ain't going, are you?"

"I dunno. I have to ask my gramma. Did you get invited?"

"Naw. I wouldn't go if I was. They only invite us poor kids for one reason: to have somebody to talk about. We ain't the same as them. We don't belong."

"Why would they talk about us?"

Billy sneered. His missing tooth made his sneer seem really ugly. His voice was mad sounding. "Open your eyes and take a look at yourself. Your pants are patched a zillion times, your shirt's too big for you, you wear shitkickers for shoes, you carry lard and sugar sandwiches for lunch so you can't never trade, you talk like a hillbilly, you ain't got no manners, and your breath stinks. Not to mention buck teeth that stick out, and jug ears. Who'd want you around, lessen it was to talk about? When they feel sorry for you, it makes them feel good about not being like you."

"Well, I don't care. I ain't never been to a birthday party of a rich kid, and I'm going. They can talk about me all they want. It don't hurt me none."

"You're dumb"

"You're dumb too. I gotta go."

I took off towards the wooded ravine, a shortcut. Before I got out of sight, I looked back. Billy was still standing there, watching me.

****

"Hi Sammy," said gramma. "You're late from school."

"I stopped to talk to Billy," I said, and could have bit my tongue right off. Billy said it was OK to tell lies, because they got you out of more trouble than they got you into. I always told the truth first, and wished I hadn't. Gramma was frowning.

"I wish you wouldn't associate with him. He's no good. His whole family's no good. His dad had been in prison more years than he's been out."

"That don't matter. Billy's a good kid. He never lies to me. I like him. He's smart, and teaches me lots of good stuff. Gramma, can I go to Ramona's birthday party? She invited me today."

Her look changed from worried to hard. I knew that look. It meant she had her mind stubborn-hard made up, and Christ and all his angels couldn't change it. "No, you can't go to Ramona's birthday party."

"Aw, gee whiz, why not?"

"Don't you question me. Because I said so, that's why not."

"I ain't never been to one."

"You've been to your sisters' and your own, and that's enough."

"Well, you could at least tell me why."

"Because we ain't got no money to be giving some little rich kid a gift, if you must know. Now shut up about it. If you had a daddy that cared, it might be different, but you ain't, and that's that."

I tried to find the far-away station that played good classical music instead of the hillbilly stuff. It didn't come in good until after sundown. I threw the radio on my army cot and started beating on my thigh with my fist.

"Don't cry, don't cry, don't cry."

****

The evening of the party came. I was restless and my mind wouldn't settle down. It kept wanting me to go to that damn party. I never told Ramona I wouldn't be there. I didn't even talk to Billy about it again.

"Money," I told myself. "No damned money. No damned dad, either. Damn you, dad. What'd we do so bad that you don't want us anymore? Shit. I'm going anyway."

"Bye, gramma. I'm going out for a walk."

"Be back by dark."

"Alright."

I went directly to the street where Ramona lived, but I stopped at the corner. I watched her house from about halfway down the block. It was a nice house, with a front porch and shade trees in the front yard, and flower beds all over. It wasn't quite dark yet, but the porch light was already on. I saw kids arriving in twos and threes. All of them were carrying packages. I leaned against a tree and watched until the sun almost went down.

Shit, I can't go, I thought as I watched the other kids. I ain't got nothing to give her. I'd feel ashamed, being the only one who didn't bring a present. Billy, he'd go...if he wanted to. He don't care what they say about him. I told him I don't care either, but I do. I couldn't stand the thought of them talking about me behind my back.

They might even laugh at me. Gramma says it's all right if they shit on you, and it can even be alright if they rub it in, but if they laugh because it stinks, it's time to get fighting mad.

I closed my eyes. I could see myself in my mind's eye just the way Billy described me. Why'd you have to tell me all that stuff, Billy? I ain't never thought about it before. He's right though. Poor people look different, smell different, act different, talk different, dress different. Even if I had nice, new clothes, that wouldn't change the rest of it. Even if I had something to give her, that wouldn't change nothing. Two kids came running by. They stopped when they saw me.

"Hey, Sam! You better hurry up! You'll miss out on the ice cream and cake."

"I ain't going."

"Suit yourself," one said, and they hurried off.

Finally, after it was dark, I walked down and leaned against one of the trees in front of the house. I thought the darkness would hide me. It sounded like the house itself was laughing because there were so many kids there. I listened to them and thought I wouldn't be able to tell the difference if they was laughing at me. If I thought they were, I'd get mad and want to fight. That'd be a pretty mess. Shit. I can't go. I couldn't help it. I began to cry.

"Damn you, dad. Damn you, damn you, damn you."

Just then, the front door opened. Ramona stepped out into the light.

"Is that you, Sam? Come on in!"

Instead, I turned around and began running away. I ran all the way home, crying all the way. I slammed the door of my room behind me and fell hard into bed.

"Damn you, damn you, damn you."

Soda Jerk

My social life was nonexistent. Unless they were fat or tall, I couldn't recognize student who waved to me on the school grounds. I seldom returned their waves and, as I found out later, got a reputation as a snob.

I got my first taste of popularity with my first job. I was a soda jerk at Myer's Drugstore. Behind the marble countertop, and in front of the stainless steel array of compartments, nozzles, and tools of the trade, I reigned supreme. The afternoon crush of kids was the high point of my entire day.

"Cherry coke, lime soda, chocolate malt, lemon phosphate."

The orders came one on top of the other, and my hands flew. I always gave good measure, adding an extra bit of phosphate, extra syrup and ice cream, extra fast service. The faster I moved, the more alive I was. It wasn't long until the girls found out I treated them the best of all.

"Oh, Sammy, I just love the way you make my malteds."

"Sammy dear, can I have some extra ice cream in my soda?"

"You know what, Sammy? I think you're cute."

My only regret was that my popularity behind the ice cream bar did not transfer to the school ground. There, I was as lonely as ever – until three older guys got a grand idea.

"Hey Sam, you want to make a little extra cash?"

"How?"

"Steal us some cundrums."

"Some what?"

"Cundrums, rubbers."

"Naw, I don't think so."

I kept refusing until, one day, my coworker Kenny got a raise. I'd worked there longer than him, and, I thought, did the work faster and better. I felt the unfairness of it to my bones. I contacted the gang of three, and told them I was willing to reconsider. Soon, I was stealing rubbers, pipes, cigarettes, and money. During the busiest times, I'd lay the money on the till instead of ringing it up. Sneaking a few extra coins to the side of the till when I did ring it up provided an extra dollar or two a day, which I promptly spent on pinball machines.

I handed out the other stuff I stole for free, preferring to be accepted as part of the gang. One of them had an old panel truck. They would ride in front, and I got to ride in the back. One time, I got the chance to join them for real, and go on an expedition with them.

"Hey Sam, you wanna go on a watermelon expedition?"

"Sure. What do I have to do?"

"Nothing special. Just watch us, and do what we do."

That night, I was again in the back of the truck as they left on the watermelon raid.

"Where we going?"

"To the Hostetler's farm. That old son-of-a-bitch has got it coming. He shot one of our friends in the ass with rock salt last year."

Even the off chance of getting shot scared me, but I was more afraid of being thought chicken. "How come he won't shoot us?"

"He won't even know we're there. We'll take the road on the far edge of the watermelon field, turn off the lights before we get there, and climb the fence. Each one of us grabs two melons and hauls ass back to the truck. Whoever's back first helps the other ones over. Then, we do it once more. You still with us?"

"Sure," I said unconvincingly.

"Well, if you ain't, we can let you out right here."

Right here was already out in the country. I reached down for some braveness.

"Hell yes, I'm with you. I steal for you, don't I?"

"That's better. The patch is at the bottom of this hill. We'll turn out the lights and coast down."

Soda Jerk

I was the last one over the fence, and the first one back again. I held two small melons. The other three were still in the patch, bent over, thumping the big ones and choosing carefully.

"Aint'cha going back for more?" they asked me.

"Naw, I'm not very hungry."

They laughed, and went back for their final two melons.

"Anybody got a knife?" I asked when they returned.

"Whattaya need a knife for?"

"To cut the watermelon."

"Watch this."

The driver picked up a melon and smashed it into the gravel road. "You only eat the heart," he said. "Who wants to spit out seeds?"

I busted my two little ones, and even ate the part where the seeds were. I was hungrier than I thought. The road looked as if dozens of watermelons had been smashed. We drove back, gloating over our revenge.

Two days later, there was an item in the newspaper about watermelon vandals. I had never thought of myself as a vandal, not even when Bob and I broke into the haunted house. It started me thinking.

That same evening, Mr. Myers called me to his desk at the back of the store. I went through a spell of panic, and wanted to run away. I went to him though, telling myself that I didn't like the damn job anyway.

"Sam, do you like working here?"

I felt myself starting to blush. "Sure I do, Mr. Myer. I like it just fine. It's the best part of my day."

"Then what's wrong?"

Oh shit, I thought. He knows. Out loud I said, "There's nothing wrong, Mr. Myer."

"Yes, there is. I know practically to the nickel how much your register should be bringing in. It's always coming up short. Kenny's register is just fine. You aren't knocking me down, are you?"

"I wouldn't do that, Mr. Myer. You can trust me."

"I believe you. If I thought you were, I'd fire you. As it is, I'm giving you a five dollar a week raise. It's not because you deserve it, but I'm hoping it will make a better worker out of you. What you're doing, you see, is trying to buy popularity with my soda fountain. I want you to quit giving out extra portions. And I see by your waistline that you've been getting the best portions of all. It's going to stop. Do you understand me?"

"Yes, Mr. Myer."

"Then get to work."

Right then and there, I decided to quit stealing, to quit giving extra portions, and to quit taking so much for myself. I was already pot-bellied and jug-assed, and didn't want to get any fatter. They were already calling me jug butt. I had a sudden and complete feeling of respect for Mr. Myer.

There was a football game that weekend, and one of the gang wanted a pack of rubbers. He met me outside after work.

"I can't do it," I said.

"You'd better," he said.

"I'm not gonna steal anymore. Mr. Myer is suspicious. Besides, I was wrong about him. He treated me just fine. I like him a lot now, and I'm going to treat him just fine too."

"What if I tell on you?"

"Then I'll tell on you."

"Chickenshit," he said. "All three of us want to talk to you after the game on Sunday. You better have our stuff, if you know what's good for you."

His threat had a deep effect on me, but not the one he intended. What if somebody really told? I knew my gramma would go crazy. My sisters, mainly the oldest one, would despise me.

That Saturday, I went to the Lake Possum Amusement Center. Pinball machines were something I could influence, something I could sometimes control. The loud snap of a game won filled me with pride and satisfaction. The dull buss of a tilt egged me on to try again. I hit a lucky streak, and ran up a total of 24 free games. I was still playing them when it came time to be at work.

All the time I'd been playing, my mind was working on my problems. I was afraid of getting beat up if I quit the gang of three. I was afraid I couldn't resist eating all that good stuff. I was afraid of losing my popularity, especially with the girls. And I was afraid that if my register showed an immediate improvement, he would know I'd been knocking down, and would fire me anyway. I suddenly knew what I had to do. I called the drugstore. Mr. Meyer answered.

"Yes, Sam, what do you want?"

"I wanted to tell you that I quit."

"All right. Just give me a week to find a replacement."

"No, sir. I quit right now. I ain't ever coming back."

And I didn't. My old route from school took my right by the drugstore. I found a new route, and never entered the store again.

Jack Dukes

Rats

Me and my friend Billy, the one that gramma didn't want me to play with, were going rat shooting. We'd made it up at school on Friday. I was to go to his place so's gramma wouldn't know. On school days, I always made gramma wake me three times, but when I was going hunting or fishing, she didn't have to wake me up at all. As soon as the sun shone in the window, I woke up and got dressed.

I got the rifle that Uncle Carroll gave me from its place in the corner. It was only a single-shot 22 with the front sight missing, but it was more than Billy had, so I felt like the leader. He was waiting on the front steps for me. His house was practically a shack. It only had roof shingles for siding, and most of those had the sand missing so that the tar paper showed through.

Billy had a top front tooth missing. It made him kind of lisp, not like someone who couldn't talk right, but he had some trouble with his S's. Outside of that and being dirty most of time, he was a nice looking kid. He had hair the color of a red sunset, and huge freckles on his face and arms.

"Hi, Sam! Got some ammunition?"

"A whole box full. Fifty shots. I begged fifty cents from gramma for them. You ready?"

"Let's go."

Billy wanted to carry my gun. I wasn't too happy about it, but I guessed I had to do it to keep him happy. He was the best friend I had. He kept pointing the gun at streetlight and going bang. It made me nervous.

"That's nuts. You're not going to eat rats, are you? Or tin cans?"

"That's different. Those are targets."

"Well, so's the streetlights."

He had me there, so I shut up. He stopped doing it anyway, so it didn't matter anymore.

"You eat breakfast?" I asked.

"No, did you?"

"No. I'm hungry."

"Me too. Got any money?"

"No, I spent it all on bullets."

"I got a quarter. Want some chili?"

"Sure. I could eat anything."

"I got me an idea about how we can both have a bowl of chili for a quarter. You game?"

"You bet."

There was a café right near the stockyards where we were going. It stayed open all night. It wasn't very big. There were no tables, just a counter with a kitchen off to the back end. No one was there but the waitress. She was in the kitchen doing dishes. When the front door opened, it rang a bell, and she came out with two glasses of water. Billy put the gun down by his feet so as not to scare her.

"Whatta you kids want?"

"How much is chili?" he asked.

"Twenty-five cents."

"I'll have a bowl."

"Whatta you want?" she asked me.

"Nothin'."

We were sitting on the stools next to the cash register. She dished up a bowl of chili and went back to her dishwashing. She couldn't see us from the backroom. Billy crumbled all the crackers into the chili, and ate it as fast as he could. When there was only a little bit left, he poured the bowl over half-full of water, and stirred it.

"Hey, waitress," he called.

"Yeah?"

She came out, wiping her hands on her dirty apron.

"Look at this chili. There's no meat in it. You must have just dipped off the soup."

She didn't question him a bit. "I'll get you a new bowl," she said, and she did.

When she went back to the back, Billy pushed the bowl over to me. There were no more crackers, but I didn't care. I was too hungry.

"Where did you learn to do that? I asked after we were outside again. "That was really great."

"Shit, it wasn't nothing. You can make most people believe anything you want to. People are dumb."

"Just for that, you get the first shot."

"Ok, good."

The sun was up above the trees now. Billy gave me back the rifle to carry. I almost said no, but then I figured his arms were tired, and I took it.

We had to cross a manure field to get to where we were going. The field was bigger than a city block. It was tricky to walk on, especially if you didn't know where to step. You could sink in it up to your knees, and the smell of stirred-up shit was awful.

"Don't step on anything over there," I said. "That's too fresh to walk on. Over here, it's harder on top. This is where we come to dig fishing worms."

"Could I go fishing with you sometime?"

"Sure. I'll let you know the next time we go. Oh, oh. Gramma doesn't like for you and me to play together. I know! I won't tell her your real name. Uncle Carroll always takes me, and he don't know what you look like. We can pick you up somewhere along the way, somewhere away from your house."

"Sounds OK to me."

"You gotta promise not to cuss though. They don't like cussing in kids. OK?"

"Shit, yes."

The manure field ended where the grass and bushes grew too high to see over. There was just a small trail going through, and we had to push a lot of weeds out of the way. Then, we came to a ditch that drained off the manure field and ran down to the Missouri River. It was about twice as deep as we were tall, and had a lot of holes in its banks. We got to the edge of it and lay down on our bellies. I loaded the rifle and gave it to Billy.

"We gotta be real still until they come out," I whispered.

"Then shut up," he said, so I did.

The gravel was still cool from the night air, but the sun felt nice and warm on our backs. Finally, the first rat stuck its nose out from one of the holes in the bank across from us.

"Wait until there's more," I whispered.

It wasn't any time at all until about a dozen of them were clean out of their holes. They ran to the center of the ditch and started eating on what drained from the stockyards, squealing at each other, and stealing bites from whoever had the best piece. Billy took aim. Bang! One of the rats jumped up into the air and came down on its side, squealing like everything. It was kicking its legs, trying to get back on its feet. The rest of the rats disappeared, back into their holes.

"Stay real still," I whispered. "You gotta watch this."

Rats

In a few minutes, the other rats came back out. They ran to the wounded rat, surrounded it, and began eating it alive.

"Give me the gun," I whispered.

He didn't do it, so I looked at him. He was staring at the rats like he couldn't tear his eyes away. I reached over, took the gun, and loaded it. Bang! Another rat dropped, and the others went back into their holes.

"Wow!" said Billy. "I ain't never seen anything like that in my life! Boy! Does that teach me a lesson!"

"What's that?" I asked. I couldn't see any lesson in it.

"You better never show you're hurt, or you get eaten up."

"Boy, that's true!" I said.

We kept shooting until all the bullets were gone, and there were too many dead rats to count. Billy turned out to be a better shot than me. Probably because he could see better. I stood up first.

"How come your gramma doesn't like me?" he asked.

"She says you're teaching me all the wrong stuff."

"You think that too?"

"Hell no. I think you're smart. No one else shows me the kind of stuff that you do. Besides, I like learning. I want to learn everything I can about everything."

Billy laughed, and threw a rock at a dead rat. "You gotta be smart if you're poor. Or else you get eaten up, like them rats."

"How come we're poor?"

"Hell, I don't know. There's niggers and injuns and poor white trash, that's all. Ain't nobody cares about us, lessen we get in their way."

"I ain't gonna be poor when I grow up."

"That ain't so," said Billy. "Once you're poor, you're always poor, no matter how much money you got. Let's go back. I'm hungry again."

We worked our way back through the weeds, and across the manure field. All the way, I kept thinking about what he said. I thought being poor meant you had no money, but he said you can be poor even with money. I had a lot to think about.

Glasses

I was the last one left after the two grade-school softball teams finished choosing up sides. It was always this way, being the last one chosen. It still hurt, but I got used to it. I often wished nobody would choose me at all, so that I wouldn't even have to play. The truth was, I couldn't see well enough to play, but I didn't know it at the time.

Jack Dukes

My mother might've suspected. We were walking to Gramma's house one night. Along the way, our dog disappeared. Halfway down the last block, my mother started calling for him.

"Did you see where he went to?"

"No."

"Oh, wait. There he is. See?"

I looked back towards the intersection that she was staring at. I couldn't see the dog under the intersection streetlight.

"No, I don't see him."

"Well, for goodness sakes. There he is, right under the light. Don't you see him?"

"Oh yeah, I guess I do," but I really didn't. It wasn't right in my family to admit to anything being wrong. That always cost money. Unless the ailment was obvious to everyone, you kept it to yourself.

It was my turn at bat. I didn't see the ball coming until it was almost there. I swung on instinct and connected for a bunt.

"Run! Run! Run!" they all screamed.

Glasses

I threw the bat, narrowly missing the catcher, and took off at full steam for first base. Halfway there, my right foot got caught behind my left heel and tripped me. I was also pigeon-toed.

I lay there, trying to decide whether to get up and show my shamed red face, or to lie there and pretend I was hurt to gain their sympathies. Honesty won. I got to my feet and headed for the outfield. The rest of the team was coming too. Mine had been the last out. No one spoke to me at all.

****

Uncle Carroll was to take me and my buddy Pete squirrel hunting. I was excited. All the men in my family were hunters and loved their guns. I knew how to use my single-shot 410 gauge shotgun on close-by, stationary targets, but this was my first chance to go real, live hunting.

"Hey, Pete. Do you think we're going to shoot anything?" I asked.

"Sure. You bet! I'll betcha we shoot a lot of things. You ever been hunting before?"

"Naw, not really. They always said I was too young."

"Betcha I get a squirrel before you do."

"No bet," I said. "You're probably a better shot than I am."

"Yeah, I probably am."

Carroll left us two boys beside a ravine that separated us from the oak woods. He went to explore another area. Suddenly Pete whispered in an excited croak, "There's a bluejay! Wanna shoot it?"

"Where?"

"There on the oak, just beside the broken branch."

"I don't see it."

"What's the matter with you? It's as plain as day."

"You shoot it then."

BLAM!

"You get it?"

"Naw, I missed. He flew up just as I stood up. Dumb bird. Did you see where it was?"

Glasses

"No, I still don't know."

"Dummy. You must be blind. Why don't you try shooting that dead limb?"

"What dead limb?"

"Never mind. Gee whiz."

Carroll, attracted by the shot, came to check out the situation. "Did you get anything?"

"Naw, just shot at some dumb old bluejay, that's all."

"Getting hungry?"

"Yeah," we chorused.

"OK. Let's go. The squirrels aren't out today. Either that, or they're wise to hunters now. Who shot?"

"I did. Sam, he can't see good enough to shoot."

"Well, that's the way it goes. He'll be better when he grows some more. Let's go now."

****

I had grown up enough to be trusted with a 20 gauge shotgun. Today, I was to go dove hunting with my friend Stanley, almost ten years older than me. Together, we walked out to the edge of town where the railroad cars had leaked grain onto the siding and the birds came in regularly to feed. Stan and I squatted in a ditch beside the tracks and waited in silence. Stan broke the silence.

"There comes some."

"Where?"

Stan pointed. "There, there's over a dozen of them." He stood up and took both shots with his double barrel. I still saw nothing.

"Why didn't you shoot?" he asked.

"I couldn't see them."

"For Christ's sake. I've only got one good eye, and I can see better than you."

I felt humiliated. I stood up. I felt the tears coming, and tried to fight them back. It almost worked. I turned my head against the breeze so that Stan would not see the welling tears. My eyes squinted against the wind. Suddenly, a tear drop shaped itself like a lens across my cornea. For an instant, I could see clearly. I saw the telephone poles, with their medal-rod steps, the clouds with their multi-dimensioned edges, the tracks disappearing around a far-away bend. Then I blinked, and the images were gone.

"I can see as good as you can," I said.

"That'll be the day," said Stan. "C'mon, let's go home. I've had enough. It's too windy to shoot good."

I didn't argue. I just left, keeping to myself the memory of my magic moment.

****

It was time to choose a sport to earn my Benton High letter. I was dismayed. Sports were out for me. They held no interest. I was not a team player. I preferred reading to running. I was ready to accept never having the big, cream-colored, red-edged B when I heard about the rifle team. Guns were something I could understand. I promptly entered the ROTC and applied for the rifle team.

A minor physical exam was required of all ROTC entrants. I flunked out on my first round, an eye test. The test was given by Sgt. Hilliards, a regular army man in charge of ROTC.

"Read the first line."

"E."

"Don't be smart. Read the whole first line."

"E is the only thing I can read."

"You're kidding."

"No, I'm not."

"Then you can't join ROTC. You've got bad astigmatism. You need glasses."

I was crushed. Glasses. My grandparents couldn't afford them. Ever since they had taken out guardianship papers, my dad had made no effort to contact us. I didn't earn enough working for Doc Bailey the veterinarian to buy them. Resignation again settled its heaviness upon my shoulders. I played hookey for the rest of the day, going to a ravine and trying to make my tears give me another magic moment. It wouldn't work, no matter how hard I tried.

That evening, I went about my chores at the pet hospital. My heart was not it, and I dawdled.

"What's the matter, son?" asked Doc.

All he got for an answer was a huge sigh. Doc left me alone until the evening was done, and then offered to drive me home. In his car, I finally opened up.

"Wish you'd have told me before," said Doc. "I've got a friend in the eye doctoring business. Can you go see him on Saturday before you come to work?"

"Sure, but I couldn't never pay him."

"Don't you worry about that. You just become the best damn shot on the team, okay?"

"I hear you, Doc. Wish I could see as good as I can hear."

"You will, son, you will. Goodnight, now."

"'Night, Doc."

****

I cried on the main street of St. Joseph, Missouri as I looked through my new glasses and saw. I saw pebbles and sand grains in the sidewalk beneath my feet. I saw the individual leaves on the trees, instead of a blurry green mass. I saw people's faces as they passed by and stared at me in wonderment. I saw the numbers on license plates and birds wheeling in the sky. By the time I had finished crying, it was as if a whole new boy had been born.

"Thank you, Doc Bailey. Thank you. Thank you. Thank you."

I was still saying it as I left the bus and entered the front door of the pet hospital, seeing everything for the first time.

Made in the USA
Charleston, SC
09 August 2012